Gift Wrapped

By

Amara Clay

Darrel Day

Birdie Hawks

Alda Helvey

P.J. Hick

Malynda McCarrick

Bartenn Mills

Magnolia "Maggie" Rivers

Emma Robuck

C. Deanne Rowe

Patrice Singleton

E.J. Whitmer

Published by Iowa Writers' Corner
Des Moines, IA

Copyright © November 19, 2016
By Iowa Writers' Corner

This book is a work of fiction. Names, places, characters, and incidents are either the product of the author's imagination, or if real, used fictitiously. Any resemblance to actual events, locales or persons living or dead is entirely coincidental.

All Rights Reserved. Except for use in any review, the reproduction or utilization of this book, in whole or in part, in any form including electronic, mechanical or other means, now known or hereafter invented, including photocopying and recording or in any information storage or retrieval system, is forbidden without the written permission of the authors.

First Printing November 2016.

ISBN-13: 978-1540525086
ISBN-10: 1540525086

Printed in the United States of America

Table of Contents

A Christmas Romance in Des Moines	1
Bishop Saves a Cat	11
Santa Secrets	31
Christmas Lights	49
A Christmas Miracle	61
An Ethnic Christmas	81
Mystic Mistletoe	87
Stealing Christmas	103
Eight Days Before Christmas	121
The 7:47 a.m. Shuttle	143
Silver Bells	159
Jingles Gets the Job Done	173

A Christmas Romance in Des Moines
By
Emma Robuck

I am so totally screwed. Those words branded on his brain cells as he saw the woman standing in the doorway.

"Julie?" he managed to croak, choking down the other words fighting their way to the top of his vocal cords. He'd been looking for her since last Christmas. And now he'd found her under these circumstances.

Was this her, though? His initial reaction was instant recognition but there was something about this girl. Something different. More maturity, a strength he hadn't noticed last year.

The beautiful brunette holding open the ice-covered screen door blinked at him. Then her eyes grew wide and she sighed deeply. As she stepped back, she murmured, "Nate, come in."

Nate stepped carefully from the slick porch and couldn't help comparing how the ice storm coated the world while his inner storm coated his brain with ice. It was so hard to think clearly with her this close. He'd been looking for her for so long.

"How did you find me?"

Nate watched those beautiful lips move and remembered how much pleasure they had given him last Christmas. From seeing her across the bar to getting a hotel room for the night together, he had been so struck by her. Smitten from the start. She was like a magnet to his steel, irresistible, such a strong attraction. She had been his from that first moment.

He remembered the gift he had for her. Seth had called him from overseas, asking Nate to pick it up from the jeweler's. "My flight's going to be delayed and I won't get in until Christmas morning. The jeweler will be closed by then," Seth had told him. "Please, Nate, you're going to Des Moines anyway. You could take the box with you. Her name and address will be on it, so you shouldn't have any trouble. I'll call the store and let them know you're coming to pick up the ring so they'll let you take it."

Nate had agreed, and now he handed Julie a gold-wrapped package tagged with her name. The gold metallic ribbon had gotten a little mashed down on his trip from Chicago to Des Moines.

"This is from Seth."

Her face relaxed a little at the mention of the name and again Nate's brain reiterated how screwed he was.

"Uh, he said not to open it until he gets here."

Julie turned the gift over in her hands, then set it on the glass and chrome coffee table in front of an overstuffed maroon couch. A nice fire was burning in the fireplace, and the flames flickered light around the darkening room.

Nate chose the armchair nearest the warm fire and shivered a little when he sat down. The storm outside seemed to be getting worse. He really should head on over to his folks' house, but he had to straighten this out with Julie first. He couldn't just walk away and leave her to his boss.

He watched her get settled on the couch with her gorgeous brown hair that shone in the firelight and her beautiful face, and he recalled the way she giggled that sent chills through him. Not in a bad way but like she was his and he was home.

But now that hair and face and laugh belonged to Seth, his boss. Apparently, in the year since Nate had forgotten to get her phone number, no matter how many times he went back to that bar and couldn't find her, Seth had found her and was now going to marry her. Damn, why hadn't he gotten her phone number?

It wasn't fair that Seth found her. And the thing was, he couldn't take her away from Seth because it might cost him his job. Nate loved his job and truly didn't want to lose it. He had to work this out with Julie before he left tonight. Seth could understand and forgive a lot from Nate, but it would be a big mistake on Nate's part to not let him know about last Christmas with Seth's soon-to-be fiancée.

The wood popped in the fireplace, drawing Nate back to the present and Julie.

"Julie." Nate reached over and touched her hand. "I need to explain…" He stopped and sat there for a moment. How could he explain why he crawled out of that hotel room bed and left her there alone?

He'd awakened and looked over at her and saw comfort and love and forever. It was that last part that had scared him to pieces. His brain shattered, and his heart thudded fast and heavy in his chest like a hundred booted men chasing him down a hallway. He'd actually worked up a sweat as he quickly and as silently as possible threw his clothes on. He'd taken one last look at her lying in the bed as he slipped out the door. Fear had punched him in the gut again. He had to get away.

The wind blew outside and the old house creaked under its thick coating of ice. Julie looked up at him and he saw the confusion and mistrust in her face. He still felt a little of the panic he'd experienced before he snuck out that night a year ago, especially now while he was sitting across from her. But he owed her an explanation and he needed things to be okay between them. He had to say something. His palms sweaty, he stood and moved over to the couch, sitting next to her.

"Julie, I tried to find you. I went back to that bar again and again. I asked everyone and no one knew you." But still, he wasn't addressing the central issue. Why he had sex with her and then crept out like a thief? This was so difficult. He'd rather climb Mount Everest than have to do this, and he was afraid of heights. "I am so sorry for—"

A strong gust of wind rocked the house and the lights flickered and went out. Total darkness except for the fireplace. Julie gave a little yelp and Nate moved closer, putting his arm around her automatically. He felt her lean into him for a moment and that brought back comfortable feelings, sensual feelings. Possessive feelings he had no right to have. She was Seth's now. She seemed to realize this too because she stiffened and sat up straight. His stomach dropped.

"Julie, we need to talk about that night. I need you to understand—"

A shrill wail came from another room and then it was joined by a second one. Julie gasped and shot up off the couch, running into the next room before Nate could ask her what was wrong.

Maybe it was an animal. Maybe she needed help. There were no more noises, but still... Julie was gone for a while, and just as Nate decided to make his way in the dark to find her, she walked back into the living room holding two little bundles, one in each arm.

It took Nate a moment to realize they were babies. It was brought home when one cried again. Julie crossed the room and put the babies in his arms. He'd never held a baby before, preferring to keep his distance from the powdery, baby-lotion-smelling, squirmy, blanketed beings. What if he dropped one? It would break then she'd be pissed at him.

"I can't—" he protested and tried to thrust them back at her.

"Just hang on to them for a minute. It won't kill you. I'll bring the bassinette out here by the fireplace so they can stay warm. With the lights out, the fireplace is the only source of heat." Julie turned and was gone into the other room before he could say anything.

The bundles started squirming and he looked down to see what they were doing, mentally begging Julie to hurry. Balancing one bundle of blankets carefully on his lap, he moved the blankets of the other one around and saw a beautiful tiny face. The little eyes met his. He felt such a swell of emotion that he really did almost drop it.

Had Seth met Julie just after the night Nate and Julie had spent together? The bundled blankets looked little so these babies weren't very old.

Those old feelings of heavy footsteps chasing him down the hallway came back into his chest. The panic was overwhelming. She shouldn't have left him here with these little baby things. He needed to go. The panic was making his heart race and his mouth dry.

He would give Julie back the babies and escape to his car. Then he'd call Seth and tell him he'd delivered the gift and congratulate him on fatherhood. No wonder Seth was in a hurry to get married.

The bundle on his lap wiggled. He dropped his free left arm down to steady it and brushed the blanket aside to reveal another precious, tiny, beautiful face. Again emotion punched him in the gut and he felt the need to get up and run. Run out to his car and go to his parents' house and never get involved with anyone again.

That's great, Nate. Go running to Mommy. Come on, be a man. Face it like a man. You are twenty-five years old, not five. Act like it.

Julie came back into the room pushing a white wicker basket on wheels.

"I see you're getting acquainted." She pushed the basket over near the fireplace and took the blanket-wrapped baby off his lap. He held out the second one but instead of taking it, Julie uncovered the first one. "This little miss is Jacindelle. Isn't she beautiful?"

He nodded, his heart thudding as he held the other one out again. Random thoughts started bouncing around his brain like a bunch of superballs. Even though he was afraid to hold them, they were cute babies. Why hadn't Seth said anything about kids? Did he think he could marry someone and just magically appear with babies? He wouldn't try to hide them, would he? You know, put them up for adoption and pretend they never happened. He wouldn't dare do that. Julie wouldn't let him do that.

Julie put Jacindelle into the basket and then reached for the other baby. She handled them so easily and he could feel the love radiating from her. She was a good mother, and she would make a great wife. If he hadn't screwed up, if he had stayed in that hotel room and not let the emotions rule him and make him run out the door, this could be his.

His wife, his children, his marriage. Strangely, it didn't sound so bad. No panic but then it was pretty unlikely. She would be engaged to Seth by this time tomorrow. Nate would spend the rest of his life looking for someone like Julie and probably never find her.

Removing the blanket, Julie leaned in closer. "This little one is Nathaniel." She looked into Nate's eyes. "I named him after his father." Then she put the infant in his arms again.

He looked at the baby, then he looked at Julie, then back at the baby again. Suddenly it struck him. This was his child. These little babies were his children.

Oh shit, these babies were his.

Oh my gawd, these were his children.

He felt the panic return in full and he stood up. Just as he was about to shove the baby into Julie's arms and run, he remembered she was engaged to Seth. Seth would be raising Nate's babies. Or more likely, he would talk Julie into giving them up for adoption. Nate couldn't allow that. Either option.

He was their father and he would be part of their lives whether Seth liked it or not. He hugged little Nate, clutching him hard to his chest. No way these babies were going anywhere away from him.

He cleared his throat. "Uhh, does Seth know about the babies?"

Julie blinked. "Of course. He's been very supportive. Speaking of Seth, why did he give you my gift, anyway? Isn't he gonna be there tomorrow?"

She wandered over and picked up the gift. "He's the reason I let you through that door. He explained how a guy feels and that it was probably fear and panic that made you leave that morning. I took it personally at first, like a rejection of me."

She gestured toward the baby in his arms. "When I found out I was pregnant and that it was twins, he was very supportive. I wished a hundred times I could call and share this with you but I didn't even know your last name. The gift of these children was the best thing that anyone could ever give me."

Nate's heart dropped. Seth knew about the babies and apparently didn't care they were not his. He was still willing to take them on. That would make equal time with them harder still for Nate. The strain on their professional relationship would eventually be too much for either of them to handle. Damn, he really liked this job.

Nate watched Julie look at the name tag on the beribboned golden box.

"Say, this tag says this is for Julie Armstrong."

"That's you, isn't it?"

Julie shook her head. "I'm always getting mail for her. She lives at the same address but on the west side of town."

She put the box back down on the coffee table. "I've never actually met her but her parents bring my mail over and I give them any of hers that was delivered here. She works in Chicago somewhere so thank goodness it doesn't happen that often."

Nate patted the baby on the bottom in what he hoped was a comforting gesture. The jeweler had given him the wrong one. So what had happened to this Julie's ring? And how preposterous were the chances that this Julie and the other Julie, both in Des Moines, were supposed to get rings from the same jeweler in Chicago?

So what was this Julie's last name? He cleared his throat. He had another question first. "You asked if Seth was going to be there tomorrow. Where is he supposed to be going? He's in Switzerland."

Julie blinked, her eyebrows furrowed. By her frown, he could tell she was confused as well. "What would Seth be doing in Switzerland?"

"He's visiting family. He didn't tell you?"

"Are we talking about my brother, Seth McDonald? Because his family is my family, and they're not in Switzerland."

"Your brother? Wait, you're not dating Seth Collins?"

"No, but I bet Julie Armstrong is." Julie smiled.

Nate plopped back down on the couch, clutching little Nate to him again. He was trying to sort it out. Seth was dating a girl named Julie, whose parents lived here in Des Moines and happened to have the same address of the girl Nate slept with last

Christmas. This was kind of crazy. It was like one of those Christmas miracles that people talk about. So he was at the wrong house, but really at the right house. So right.

How many times had he regretted leaving that morning a year ago? How many times had he dreamed about Julie? How many times had he longed to find her and make sure she was the one and make it real? Now he could.

But only after he explained it to her. Only after she forgave him for being a shit and running out on her.

His cell phone rang. He dug it out of his pocket and glanced at the screen. It was Seth. Oh, crap. He was in trouble now. It seemed he would spend his whole night explaining. If he was lucky, his explanations would be good enough.

Holding a finger up to Julie, he answered the phone. "Hey, Seth."

"Nate, don't deliver the gift. Throw the damned thing away. I never want to see it again or hear that lying, cheating bitch's name again."

"What happened, man? You sound upset."

"I just called the bitch to find out if she got the gift yet and a man answered. A man that basically ripped me a new one for harassing his girlfriend. I got Julie on the phone and the bitch blubbered while she told me she got back together with an old boyfriend."

"Oh no. I'm sorry Seth. You were really serious about this one. What can I do to help?"

"Just get rid of that gift and never mention her name again."

Nate smiled and winked at Julie. "I know just what to do with it. Thanks, man. See you on Monday."

He did know exactly what to do with it. He could give it to his Julie and if she didn't like the idea of another woman's ring for her engagement ring, then they could sell the darned thing and use the money for a down payment on a decent house. Hopefully one that didn't lose power in an ice storm.

Nate hung up the phone, put little Nate in with his sister and crossed the room to Julie. He took the package from the coffee table, ripped off the nametag and handed it to her.

"Julie, one year ago when I met you, I knew I'd met the one. The one woman for me, the one that I could be happy with, the one to marry and have children with. And it scared the hell out of me. So I ran. I've regretted it since, every single minute. I cannot tell you how many times I went back to that bar looking for you and couldn't find you."

He dropped to one knee, sweating like he'd run a marathon. His heart beat so fast, he wondered if he was having a heart attack. Swallowing, he took a deep breath. "Julie, I don't ever want to lose you again. I want you to marry me and I want to raise those babies with you and maybe make some more."

He pointed to the box. "This is not what I would have picked out for you. We can get a different ring later but for now, please wear this one as a symbol of my undying love. Please forgive me and say yes."

The grandfather clock in the hall chimed midnight as she opened the box to see the jeweled miniature Christmas tree, and sitting atop it was a huge heart-shaped diamond with an emerald on one side and a sparkling ruby on the other. He pulled the box out of her hands and held the ring up to her.

"Merry Christmas, my one and only Julie. Please marry me."

She nodded and he slipped the ring onto her finger. The tears running down her cheeks reflected the light from the fire with as many sparkles as the diamond on her finger.

Bishop Saves A Cat
By
Bartenn Mills

The day after Christmas and all through the house not a creature was stirring except for himself.

Bishop gave a half snort and finished tying his shoe laces. After two days, the wind had finally stopped. Just in time because the case of cabin fever and boredom that was stifling him had erupted into an uncontrollable volcano. Not that he wanted to get called in to work, Garfield Falls had enough murders for a town hardly big enough to be called a city, but the four walls of his tiny rental house were closing in on him.

He secured his handgun in his back holster and shrugged on a jacket. The relentless wind had pushed snow up against the back door and even a hard shove couldn't get it open.

Foolish to go out jogging with snowbanks crowding the sides of the road. But there was a convenience store only a mile away. There and back, then a beer to help him sleep.

Bishop headed out the front. The twilight of late afternoon cast a gray tone to the world. Only his sidewalk had been shoveled. The cold nipped at him. After a token stretch, he jogged in the street past the cluster of low-rent houses. Even the heavy snow of the past week hadn't covered the hopelessness of the homes. Half-open curtains revealed tired families staring at flickering images on television screens beneath the glow of Christmas tree lights.

He noticed a pair of juveniles hovering near a broken fence that divided two yards. One had a stick and with swift prods poked at something between the wood boards and a garbage can.

A hiss and yowl answered back at him.

Bishop broke the rhythm of his stride.

A cat, they were poking at a cat.

"Hey!" Bishop stopped.

The one with the stick turned around. Anger hung on him like lights on a Christmas tree. His face said that he was early teens but his attitude said all grown up.

"Get lost old man."

The boy bounced the stick in his hand. Although tall and heavy for fourteen or fifteen, the weight wasn't from muscle. That would come in a few years. So would the street smarts – like being able to tell an off-duty police officer from a jogger. Or mistaking a man in an old jacket for a vagrant roaming the streets.

The stick bounced again and the kid took a step forward. Tension crackled in the cold night air as he and Bishop faced off. The younger boy hung back, his eyes large in the twilight. Bishop didn't need this. All he wanted was for them to leave the cat alone.

Mistaking his hesitancy for fear, the teenager smiled. Before Bishop could speak, before either could move, the cat solved the stand-off. With attention diverted and the stick no longer prodding him, the cat bolted, dashing between its tormentor's legs.

The smaller boy grabbed at the animal, catching it by the tail and holding it up. The cat hissed and yowled, swiping at the air in and attempt to get free. The bigger boy looked away from Bishop and laughed at the cat.

Bishop moved and the fight was over before the kid knew it had started. Speed plus mass pushed the teenager against the wooden fence. The stick was out of his hands and tossed into a snowbank before he could even react. In a heartbeat the hooligans realized that Bishop was no street bum easily rolled for smokes and small change. Fear flashed across their faces. In desperation, the smaller boy tossed the cat. As it flew through the air at Bishop, both boys ran.

Angry and snarling, claws extended, the animal hit Bishop's chest and dug in. Sharp nails pierced through the thin fabric of his jacket, ripping deep enough to touch flesh. Bishop flinched.

Instead of flinging the animal aside, he held it closer. "Shhh, shhh." His voice dropped into a soothing rumble. "It's alright. It's alright. They're gone." He glanced around to be sure they were indeed gone.

"You're alright." The cat's heart pounded hard enough for Bishop to feel it through his jacket. He waited, holding the animal, stroking its head until the wild scratching stopped and its heartbeat slowed to the tempo of a waltz.

Finally he set the animal on the ground. Its legs wobbled beneath it and the cat collapsed on the cold cement. Bishop stared down at the ugly beast. Its tail hooked the wrong way and one leg seemed limp. The ears tipped toward him and the eyes watched him, but it didn't lift its head. If left in the cold by morning it would be dead.

The last thing he wanted was to be responsible for another living thing.

Carefully lifting the animal, Bishop nestled it inside his jacket. Maybe his mother would take it, or one of his sisters.

Maybe Sonny needed a cat.

The idea warmed him. What said Father of the Year more than giving your kid a pet?

Using one hand to hold the cat steady, Bishop turned back toward his house and ran full out. He'd have to take it to the vet first. Claire would never let a filthy animal into her house.

Bishop set the cat on the seat of his parked car and dashed inside, where he changed his light jacket for a winter coat and grabbed his wallet. The message light on his land line flashed at him and he picked up.

"I didn't hear from you yesterday." Priscilla's unmistakable voice, high-pitched and more than a little nasal, hesitated in that open-ended fishing-for-information way.

Of course he hadn't called on Christmas. She would have asked him over; he would have gone. That would have meant giving her a present. And if he gave her a present on Christmas, she would have expected it to be a ring. He'd been down that road before. No, better to just ignore the holiday entirely.

"Well, I guess you're busy. But if you're free later, I'm making pasta for supper. Any time after eight works just fine."

After eight. That meant the offer was for more than supper. He should pick up a bottle of wine.

When he got back to the car, the cat didn't move from the passenger's seat. Not even the flick of a tail. Maybe it was dead. Then the eyes blinked and it gave a weak meow.

"Hungry?"

Bishop scrounged beneath the seat and found several coffee cups, one with a few dregs of fluid in the bottom. The animal eagerly lapped up the dark liquid. Food was not so easy to come by, but he finally found the crusts from some sandwich, origin unknown. The cat didn't seem to care and eagerly swallowed the dry bread as if it was a feast, even giving Bishop a warning growl should he think of taking the morsel away.

Bishop figured if he hurried, the vet's office would still be open. He was almost right. The outside light flicked off just as he pulled into the parking lot. He went up and rapped on the door anyway.

A woman peeked out and shook her head. He lifted the cat from beneath his coat, hoping that it looked pitiful enough to win her over. It did.

Even as she opened the door, she told him they were closed. Before she could change her mind, Bishop stepped inside.

"I think it's hurt." He handed it to her.

She sighed. "Your cat?"

While she held the beast with one hand, she deftly ran the other over its body. It tried to pull away, its paws reaching out toward Bishop, but Bishop shoved his hands into his pockets to keep from taking the cat back.

"No. I found it while I was jogging."

"Feral cat?"

He shrugged. How would he know? If it belonged to the two kids tormenting it, he wasn't taking it back to them.

"Underfed. You're lucky it's not summer or it would be full of fleas and worms. Still could be. Tail's broke." She looked up at Bishop, her face hard and her eyes cold. "I don't have room for another feral cat. Especially not a black one. People think they're bad luck and won't take them. If you want to pay, I'll fix it up and get you some quality food, otherwise we'll euthanize it in the morning."

*****

An hour later he was back in the car with a clean animal and fifty dollars' worth of supplies. Not what he had planned.

Instead of staying on the passenger's seat, the beast climbed up and onto Bishop's shoulder, and then wrapped itself around his neck like a soft scarf. After a few moments of purring, it slept.

Bishop drove north and west to a nice part of town where row after row of little ranch houses had been planted to grow young families. An occasional split-level broke the monotony. Claire had gotten the house in the divorce settlement. He still paid half the mortgage. At the time it seemed like a fair deal. All he'd wanted was out. But seeing it there with the Christmas lights, snow-topped and postcard perfect, he forgot about the arguments and the lies and the anger and only remembered the dreams.

A blue Mazda sat in the garage, Claire's SUV in the driveway. Bishop parked on the street. The house lights were off. He could leave the animal in the garage; it would be warm enough until morning. He tucked the cat beneath his coat and went around to the back. The cat peered out, its soft fur brushing his face. Then it bumped his chin with its head.

Bishop fingered his key chain. If no one had changed the locks, he could let himself in. It would only take a moment to leave the cat and the bag of supplies. Maybe make a Santa face on the bag so Claire would know it had been him.

No one had changed the lock. Without turning on a light, he maneuvered past the tiny entry to the kitchen. How many times had he let himself into the sleeping house? A pan of cinnamon rolls, covered with a thin cotton cloth, sat rising on the counter. By morning they'd be ready to pop into the oven, hot and fresh for breakfast.

Someone flicked on the bathroom light. He shifted the cat, tucking it inside his coat where it curled itself around his torso, its tail tickling his back. The light went out, soft footsteps came toward the kitchen. Moonlight illuminated her path, moonlight made him a shadow.

When she finally saw him, she pulled back.

"Vinnie." It was a soft hiss. "How did you…?" She didn't finish, she knew how he'd gotten in. "What are you doing here?"

"I brought Sonny a present."

"You could have done that yesterday."

What did she expect him to say? He hadn't. No excuses, he just hadn't.

"Fine. Get out before you wake him." Small, bare feet raced down the hall, the slap of flesh to wood. Too late.

"Daddy, daddy."

Sonny brushed past his mother's long nightgown and grabbed Bishop's legs.

"Hey big boy, what are you doing up?" Bishop bent down and scooped Sonny into his arms. When had he gotten so big? What was he now? Six or seven? Bishop had to do the math, subtracting the year Sonny was born from the current year. Seven? Did seven year olds like cats?

Trapped between them, the cat meowed with displeasure. It forced its nose out of the folds of Bishop's coat, its head and ears following.

"No. Vinnie, no."

Bishop locked his gaze on Claire. "You always said he needed a pet."

"A fish, or a hamster, not a cat." Her lips set in a straight line. "No."

Sonny's hands quivered. Tentative fingers reached out to touch the dark fur on the animal's head. But the cat pressed itself against Bishop and with a hiss, it bared its teeth. Heedless of the warning, Sonny's hand kept moving toward the animal and was rewarded with a sharp claw. For an instant the child froze, staring at the thin lines of red that blossomed on his skin. Then he burst into tears.

Twisting, pushing, Sonny reached for his mother.

A cry came from the bedroom. Bishop had forgotten about the new baby, not his child but Claire's and her new husband's.

"See what you've done."

Sonny's head pressed into her shoulder and she stroked his hair. "Shh, you'll be fine." Over the child's head she glared at Bishop. "Get out."

"I just wanted—"

"I know what you wanted. You wanted to play at being a father. Well, you're a day late. Christmas was yesterday." Her eyes shot anger that hit him like an arrow through the heart. "And I know that it was your mother that bought the train set."

He couldn't deny it.

"Get out."

A sleepy man carrying a baby appeared in the kitchen doorway, the infant's face scrunched up and red with screaming. The man, Claire's new husband, frowned at seeing Bishop. "What's going on?"

"Vinnie is leaving."

He might have stayed, argued about the cat, but something told him that he would lose. Retreat seemed the better option. Juggling the cat in one hand and opening the door with the other, Bishop let himself out. Back in the car the animal pressed itself against the far door. Its yellow eyes glared at Bishop.

"Yeah, that didn't go as planned. Looks like I'm stuck with you. For now anyway."

The day after Christmas might have had more sunlight than the day before, but darkness had already stretched into the nooks and crannies. It was after seven, not too soon to show up at Priscilla's. They could eat early, stay up late.

The 24/365 convenience store carried wine. The boxes were cheapest. But that wouldn't impress Priscilla. As Bishop studied the row of liquor bottles, a big kid strutted in, a smaller kid following. Bishop recognized them from before but they didn't even look his direction. Instead the smaller one headed down the candy aisle while the big one headed for the coolers of pop and beer.

Hard to watch them both. The clerk kept her eye on the larger one so Bishop watched the other. He wasn't much older than Sonny. Certainly he shouldn't be out roaming the streets.

The boy picked up two candy bars, clumsily attempting to palm one and drop it into his pocket. Then he deliberately disturbed the boxes, knocking several onto the floor.

"Oops, sorry."

While the clerk scurried to straighten the mess, the kid stood and watched her, his arms dangling at his sides.

The tell-tale whoosh of breaking suction as a cooler door opened caught Bishop's attention. He glanced over in time to see the older boy slide a can of beer into his pocket. A smirk on his face, the kid scanned the store to see if anyone was watching.

Bishop was. He made hard eye contact. The kid smiled, daring Bishop to say anything. He wasn't child services, and he wasn't on-duty. He didn't need this.

"Maybe you should put that back."

"Yeah, whatever." The kid pulled the can of beer out of his pocket and let it drop onto the floor. After one bounce it rolled until it hit a display and thudded to a stop. "Come on, Josh."

Obediently, the younger boy followed.

"Brats." The clerk muttered under her breath.

As Bishop paid for his wine, he watched the two boys pass his car. From the darkness, the cat came at the window, claws extended, teeth bared. Both boys jumped at the sudden movement.

"Shii— " the younger one swore, but the older one slapped his hand against the car window. When the cat ducked back into the shadows, the kid laughed. Bishop watched until they disappeared down the street.

"Know them?" he asked the clerk.

"Yeah, they live down by the lake. Little brats. They came in here a few hours ago with a government check, the older one claiming to be Duane Chester. Like I couldn't see that had been stolen."

"What happened?"

"They ran off when I suggested we call their parents."

"And the check?"

She shook her head. "I guess the big one took it with him."

*****

It was eight by the time Bishop got to Priscilla's apartment in the old Garfield Falls Hotel. It wasn't the penthouse, but it wasn't the bottom floor either. She was a woman on her way up. They'd met on opposite sides of a case. The jury had found in his favor, and then he had found himself enjoying her favors on what had now become a regular basis.

When she opened the door, she was still in her work clothes, her crisp white blouse and pencil skirt professional yet feminine. She leaned into him and took the bottle of wine. He tasted her lips.

Instead of sweet sugar, he tasted her lingering anger. If he wanted to stay, he would have to work at it.

The holly wreaths were gone, the Christmas tree was already down, and the sofa had been pushed back to where it belonged. You'd never know it was only one day after the holiday.

Priscilla closed the door and something brushed the back of his leg. Bishop glanced down. How'd the cat get out of the car without him noticing? He scooped up the animal. Maybe he could salvage Christmas after all.

"I hadn't wanted to just spring it on you." He smiled and dropped his voice, letting it rumble in that deep register he knew women liked. "Merry Christmas."

"A cat?" She had no choice but to take it as he shoved it into her arms. "You brought me a cat? For Christmas?"

"Something to keep you company."

The verdict was out. All he needed was the cat to be charming and she'd go for it. Instead the beast hissed and took a swipe at her I've-never-done-manual-labor hands with their perfectly manicured nails. She held the animal at arm's length.

"You thought that I'd like a cat for Christmas?"

No, he'd thought she'd like a ring and a promise; that's why he'd stayed away.

"This is just what I've been saying—"

He couldn't recall her ever talking about cats.

"—you never think of anyone but yourself."

When had she told him that?

"I can't take care of a cat."

Then what made her think that she could handle life with a homicide detective?

"I'm sorry, but dinner is cancelled." She shoved the cat back at Bishop.

He hadn't really cared about the free meal; it was the dessert afterward that he was in the mood for. The cat curled into his arms, pressing against his chest harder than an EMT doing CPR. For a moment Bishop considered making empty promises, but that would just string the relationship out until he had another ex-wife and even more support payments.

He'd keep the cat.

And the wine.

*****

His car hadn't even had time to get cold. He dumped the cat unceremoniously onto the passenger's seat. They exchanged glares.

"One night, then you're off to my mother's."

The cat turned away from him and gazed out the window. Its ears twitched forward. A squad car, lights flashing but siren silent, raced past headed toward the south. The cat climbed onto the dash staring out the window after the lights as interested in the disappearing squad car as Bishop was.

Bishop flicked on the police radio. Whatever call the squad had been answering had already been broadcast. Finding nothing but the crackle of dead air, he called in to dispatch.

"Bishop? I've been trying to reach you at home."

That meant a dead body. She gave him the address. Near his house. He had to push the cat off the dash to see well enough to drive.

"You didn't have any missing cats called in?"

The woman on the other end snorted. "Not enough crime for you?" There was the rustle of papers. "None."

The cat jumped back onto the dash but stayed on the passenger's side just out of reach.

"You wouldn't want a cat?"

"Nope."

"I found a black stray. If anyone calls in looking for it, I'm looking to get rid of it." Bishop glanced over at the cat. Its tail flicked, but it kept its eyes forward.

*****

Bishop tried to leave the cat in the car, cracking a window so it would have some air, but the beast slid out faster than he could close the door. Good, maybe it would run away and he wouldn't have to take care of it. But the animal followed him, gingerly stepping in the footprints Bishop left in the snow. When they got close to the body, the cat sat and watched.

At first glance it looked as if a man had curled up near the trunk of a tree and gone to sleep. The ragged clothes, the unwashed stench now mingling with the smell of death said the man lived on the streets. An empty whiskey bottle lay nearby.

Bishop's heart sighed. Maybe they'd find out his name. Maybe they'd find a wife or child left behind. Most likely he would join the stack of unresolved deaths Bishop kept in the bottom drawer of his desk at the station.

"Who found him?"

A large officer nodded toward a woman holding a small fluffy dog in her arms, rocking it like a baby.

She gave Bishop her name. "I thought he was sleeping." Her gaze kept wandering back toward the dead man. "I was just going to leave a few treats for his cat. But when I called to him, he didn't move, and Caesar here started barking."

The dog sniffed at Bishop and yipped. Yeah, he probably smelled like a cat. He'd forgotten about the cat. Where was the beast?

Bishop glanced around. The black cat had pushed itself between the dead man's arms. Now instead of looking as if he was sleeping, it looked as if the man was trying to protect the cat with his body.

Bishop pushed the thought aside and focused on the woman in front of him.

"You know his name?"

"Duane something. Said it was his father's name." Tears swelled up in her eyes. "We were so busy with family yesterday. And with all the snow. I never thought." The dog squirmed and she sat it down, keeping hold of the leash. "Did he freeze to death?"

Normally Bishop would think so, but the cat…

"Is that his cat?"

"Yes. His name is Caesar. It's my dog's name, too. That's how I got to know Duane. We were both yelling Caesar, Caesar. I found his Caesar, he found mine." She stared over at the body. "He wasn't here before."

No, the cat hadn't been, he'd been with Bishop. And before that he'd been trying to hide from two boys and a big stick.

The snow around the corpse had been trampled, first by the woman and her dog, then the officer first on the scene. That would tell him nothing. Bishop walked a wide circle around the body. It wasn't hard to find the wallet where it had been tossed aside, its black leather distinct against the white snow. An expired and faded license read Duane Chester.

Bishop looked up. Attracted by the flashing lights of several squad cars, a crowd had started to form. Like flames drawing moths, as each car had arrived it had pulled more people in. Bishop studied the crowd. At the front of the yellow police tape that kept the onlookers back stood the two boys. He'd rather interview his ex-wife than someone underage.

"I want to talk to them." He gestured toward the boys.

A uniformed officer brought them over to Bishop's car. They left the car door open and the heater running.

Bishop let the younger one sit on the edge of the seat, his legs dangling out the door. The older one stood several feet away next to Officer Jefferson.

Positioned between the boys, Bishop turned his attention to the younger one.

"You were out earlier. Did you come by this way?"

The boy glanced toward his friend. Or was it his older brother? Bishop shifted so that his shoulder prevented the boys from making eye contact.

"No."

Lie number one.

"Did you know Mr. Chester?"

"That bum?" The boy shook his shoulders in repulsion. "I didn't know him."

Lie number two.

"But you knew his cat?"

"Yeah, everybody knows that filthy animal. Always digging in the garbage. Somebody ought to shoot it."

Bishop liked the lies better.

"So, Josh—"

The boy looked at Bishop in surprise. He hadn't told Bishop his name.

"What were you and your brother—"

"He ain't my brother. Travis and I are half-brothers."

"What did you do with the check? The one you took from the wallet?"

"We didn't steal it. Travis has it in his pocket."

Half true.

"Hey, what are you asking him? Don't you tell him nothing, Josh."

The car heater blasted hot air on the kid's back. Since his feet didn't touch the ground, his pant cuff had pulled up, exposing the skin between pant and socks to the cold winter air, making him shiver and sweat at the same time.

"And what happened before you found the check?"

A bead of perspiration broke out on Josh's forehead.

"We were just having some fun trying to hit the cat with the stick. The old guy just got in the way."

"Shut up, Josh."

Bishop straightened. That was all he needed. The old guy got in the way so one or both of them had hit him with the stick. And when he'd stopped moving they'd stolen his government check. Then Bishop had happened by and saved the cat.

"Get that dog away from me." Travis kicked at the little dog sniffing his shoe, sending it scurrying off with a yelp.

"And you stay away from me too. I know the law. I want an attorney. I ain't done nothing."

A disheveled man, hastily dressed, his hair uncombed and sticking out in places, followed by a woman, a winter coat pulled tight over her nightgown, pushed to the front of the crowd. They would be the parents.

Bishop pulled a business card out of his pocket. It was Priscilla O'Connell's. Her home number had been scribbled on the back. He wasn't going to need it anymore. But they would need a good defense attorney. Maybe she'd win this time.

*****

Bishop took the cat home. Dawn was lifting its sleepy head when his hit the pillow. The cat slipped beneath his arm and the house didn't feel so empty. A soft purr rumbled like a lullaby.

Not until a loud pounding at the front door woke him did Bishop move. When he finally got downstairs, a disheveled man looking more like a street bum than an undercover cop was half way down the sidewalk. Bishop shook the sleep from his brain. What was Q doing here?

"Hey, man, you look like you've been up all night chasing ghosts," Bishop hollered.

"I hear that you got a cat."

The animal stuck its head out the door and stared at Q.

"And it's black! Perfect."

Q was on the porch and had the cat in his arms before the animal could flee. He ruffled the beast between the ears and Caesar took a swipe at him. But his hand was out of the way before the cat's claws found flesh. Q laughed. They batted at each other, Q making a game of it, his reflexes honed as fast as the cat's.

"Here's the thing. I've been undercover over at the Capital so I missed Christmas. You know how that goes. The ex is mad, the kid thinks I'm a jerk."

Bishop inwardly flinched.

"Then dispatch says that you found this cat and were trying to get rid of it and I think – the kid needs something to get him out of his books." Q nestled the cat in his arms. "What's its name?"

"Caesar."

"Caesar? Works for me." Q rubbed the cat's back coaxing a purr out of him. The animal was as charmed by the undercover officer as most women were. "Yeah, you like old Q."

The cat's ears flicked forward and he stared at Bishop.

They had both known he wasn't staying.

"How much?"

For an instant Bishop was stumped. He couldn't profit from a man's death.

"I'll give you the bag of cat supplies that the vet sold me and throw in a twenty, but no more. Take it or leave it."

Q's eyebrows knit in puzzlement, then he realized Bishop was going to pay him to take the animal. "Done."

Money exchanged, the cat and sack of supplies in Q's arms, Bishop closed the door. The house seemed hollow. He shrugged it off. It was just the after-the-holiday let-down. Christmas had filled up the corners with light. Now that it was over, the shadows had returned. Everything felt emptier, but it wasn't really. Everything was the same as it had been before.

His jogging shoes were by the door. He was awake. He might as well go for a run.

Santa Secrets
By
E.J. Whitmer

"Let's see…favorite color? Navy blue. Favorite non-alcoholic drink? Raspberry tea. Favorite alcoholic drink? Um…Red wine. Malbec. Favorite game? Rock Band, for sure. Best. Drummer. Ever! Favorite movie?" Zoe Osbourne chewed on her pen cap as she contemplated her answer.

"Why don't you just skip the questionnaire and ask Santa for a man this year?" Maisy Cross nudged Zoe with her hip as she set her lunch tray on the table next to Zoe.

Zoe rolled her eyes and returned her attention to the Secret Santa Questionnaire in front of her. "I'd rather he brought me some good tequila and a pint of Rocky Road," she quipped with a smirk. "Did you sign up for this, too?"

Human Resources had sent out an email regarding the first annual Secret Santa project. It was their attempt at breaking the ice between existing staff and the new staff that came along with the merger of Sumner Business Solutions and Bane Incorporated.

Maisy nodded as she chewed through a too-large bite of her turkey sandwich. "Yep. It's kind of lame, but I'm holding out hope that one of the VPs gets my name and showers me in Prada purses and artisan chocolates."

"You know there's a ten dollar maximum for each gift, right?" Zoe finished filling out her form and folded it in half.

"Maybe it's relative. Ten dollars to us simpletons. Ten thousand to the 'richies.'"

Zoe tossed a piece of lettuce at her friend and stood to leave. "As always, I admire your optimism. Sorry I can't eat lunch with you today. I have to prepare for my meeting with the new boss."

She waved goodbye and quickly bused her tray before hustling out of the cafeteria. The meeting wasn't until two o'clock and it was only noon, but Zoe wanted to triple-check her notes before triple-checking them again. The new owner of Sumner Business Solutions had requested one-on-ones with each of the department heads. She was about as anxious to meet the man as she was to eat her Nana's creamed Brussels sprouts casserole. Rumor had it he was planning on cutting staff by a third. Zoe loved her employees and had hand-selected each one of them. The thought of laying off even one person made her physically ill.

On her way back to her office, she stopped by HR to drop off her questionnaire. One of the assistants tossed the form on top of a large stack of others and handed Zoe a slip of paper outlining the rules. She turned to head back to the elevators, reading the memo as she walked.

Thank you for participating in Bane Incorporated's Secret Santa Exchange. You will receive an email from HR with two numbers. One will be your assigned number and the other will be the number of the person for whom you will be a Secret Santa. You will also receive that person's questionnaire to help you with your gift selection. The exchange will take place over the next two weeks. You may give as many gifts as you like over the course of the two weeks, but no gift may be over a ten dollar value. You are by no means required to spend all ten dollars. It's just a maximum. Please drop your gifts off at the couriers' station on the third floor with your Secret Santa Recipient's number printed clearly on the box. You may reveal yourself to your Secret Santa recipient at the Bane Incorporated Holiday Party on December 18th. Until then, keep your Secret Santa secret! Happy Holidays from HR!

A small thrill raced through Zoe as she finished reading. She loved Christmas time. The smells, the music, the anticipation of celebrating with family and friends.

She was so immersed in her reflections, she didn't notice the hard wall of muscle that stepped in her path. With a loud "oompf," she bounced off a very large chest and would have landed squarely on her bum had that chest not been attached to equally large arms perfect for catching falling women.

Zoe's heart stuttered as she stared up into the bluest eyes she had ever seen. The eyes rested below dark brows arched with concern. Her gaze traveled down a straight nose and landed on full lips. Lips that were moving.

"Miss, are you alright?" The question came out as a deep purr and sent a shiver down Zoe's body. The man was almost too good looking.

She shook her head and scrambled to correct her footing, trying desperately to ignore the firm muscle under her palms as she used the man's shoulders to help right herself.

"I'm fine," she stammered. "Thank you for catching me. Obviously, I wasn't looking where I was going." She let out a nervous chuckle as she attempted to calm her racing heart.

The man smiled down at her, clearly amused. "I'm Logan." He held out a large, well-manicured hand.

Zoe reached forward and shook his hand, surprised by the rough callouses scraping against her palm. "Zoe," she murmured. She broke eye contact and glanced down at the man's orange paisley tie. She had to give him kudos. In her experience, men with rough, calloused palms didn't often attempt to rock a paisley tie with a navy suit.

"Too much?" Logan asked, obviously noticing Zoe's intense scrutiny of his tie.

Her cheeks flushed as she quickly shook her head. "No, not at all. Very stylish." She glanced around the office floor, desperately seeking an easy way out of the awkward conversation. Luckily, Logan solved her problem without prompting.

"Well, Zoe, I hate to be rude, but I've got a conference call in a few minutes. Hopefully I'll see you around." With another polite smile and a nod, he turned and strode toward the stairwell.

Zoe watched his retreating form and couldn't help but notice how well Logan filled out his tailored slacks. Just as he reached the door, he turned back and caught her perusal of his rear end. A knowing smile slowly spread across his very masculine jaw before he turned and exited.

Zoe barely contained her embarrassed groan as she turned toward the elevators. She blamed Maisy for her corrupt thoughts. Before meeting her flamboyant coworker, she was about as chaste as a nun. Okay, maybe that was an over-exaggeration, she thought. But she definitely wasn't the type to get caught checking out a male coworker's butt.

Once safely back in her office, Zoe got to work compiling information on her employees. The new owner wanted a complete rundown on duties performed by every person on staff at Bane Incorporated. Not only was the task daunting, it pretty much spelled out "layoffs" in Zoe's mind.

She was re-reading her files for the fourth time when a knock sounded at her door. After a deep, calming breath, she called for her guest to come in.

At the first glimpse of a navy trouser, Zoe knew she was in trouble. The man who walked in the door was none other than Logan, the Adonis she'd nearly bowled over two hours earlier. For some reason, it seemed to ease her nerves a bit to see that he was just as surprised to see her as she was him.

Once the initial shock wore off, Logan smiled warmly at her and approached her desk. "Well, isn't this a surprise," he mused as he sat in one of her guest chairs. "I should have known there wouldn't be two Zoes on staff. It's a beautiful name, but not too common."

Zoe flushed at the compliment and smoothed away invisible wrinkles on her pencil skirt. "Thank you. I don't know that I have your first name in my notes. Just that I'd be meeting with a Mr. Baneford."

"I apologize for the impersonal email," he replied sincerely. "This merger happened so quickly, I'm afraid quite a bit of the internal communication was drafted and sent without much thought."

Zoe sat behind her desk and shook her head slightly, dismissing the apology. "It's no problem, really. So, how can I help you today? I've got the personnel files you requested."

"Thank you." He nodded and reached for the stack of folders. "I actually just wanted to meet the directors in person and make sure they know I'm available for questions or suggestions. I'd like to make this transition as painless as possible."

Zoe fought the urge to bite her lower lip. "May I ask, will there be layoffs?" At Logan's lifted brow, she hurried to clarify. "I realize it may be confidential, and I do respect that. Really, I just wanted you to be aware that rumors are flying that our people will be let go. And with it being the holiday season, I'm afraid some may panic."

Logan took a moment to collect his thoughts before answering. "With any merger, there may be a need for some shifting around of staff. It's not something I enjoy doing. I'm also sensitive to the fact that it is December. Nothing will be decided before the holidays."

His tone was professional and a bit cold, igniting Zoe's "Irish Fire" as her mother liked to call it. "Perfect," she replied a little too sweetly. "So we'll wait to tell people they're fired until after they've piled on debt from buying too many Christmas gifts."

Had she not noticed the slight flare of Logan's nostrils, Zoe would have assumed her response didn't faze him. He took a deep breath and looked her in the eye. "Mergers come with casualties. It's not something I enjoy doing, but it's a necessity." The words came out with more than a little bite, effectively reprimanding Zoe for her gumption without specifically saying so.

She held his gaze for a long moment before nodding. "Is there anything else you need from me?"

Logan stood and brushed his slacks. "Not at this time. I'll circle back with you once I've gone through these files." With a final glance and a slight tilt of the head, he strode through the door.

The rest of the afternoon passed slowly for Zoe. Every time she saw one of her employees, she immediately pictured him jobless, swimming in debt and eating ramen noodles. She would fight tooth and nail for each of them to keep his job, even if that meant she lost hers. Her mind set, she finished her day working on a list of reasons why each of her employees was pivotal to the success of the company.

*****

The next morning Zoe sat down at her desk, booted up her computer, and was surprised to find an email from Human Resources regarding her Secret Santa.

Good morning,

Your Secret Santa number is 23. Please double-check that any packages you receive from the couriers have your number on them.

The person for whom you are buying gifts is number 72. Please print his or her number legibly on the gifts you purchase and leave them in the courier's station on the third floor. Attached to this email you will find your person's questionnaire to help you with gift selection. Any questions may be directed to HR. Thank you.

Zoe opened the attachment and printed it off. Just as she sat down with paper in hand, her door swung open and Maisy waltzed in.

"Did you get your Secret Santa person?" she asked as she plopped down in a guest chair. "I got mine. It's totally a chick. Favorite color is pink. Favorite movie is Legally Blonde. Likes diet coke and grilled chicken salads. Ugh. Boring!"

Zoe winced sympathetically for her friend and looked down at her paper. "Well, at first glance, mine seems like a man. He likes scotch, strong coffee, John Wayne movies, lemon merengue pie, and college football."

"Ooo!" Maisy wiggled her eyebrows. "Sounds like a sexy man! So, got any ideas on your first gift?"

"I've had the list for all of two minutes, Maisy. Give me a bit."

"Yeah, yeah." Maisy rolled her eyes and stood to leave. "Well, good luck with your sexy man, Santa. If you want to trade, just let me know. You can have Barbie and I'll take Ken."

After work that night, Zoe stopped by the store and perused the aisles, looking for a present. She wanted to put a piece of herself into each of the gifts to make things a bit more personal and heartfelt. However, with her Secret Santa list, it wasn't exactly easy. How does one buy scotch for a man and somehow make it meaningful? And do it for less than ten dollars!

Inspiration struck as she wandered through the movie section. He had said he loved John Wayne movies. One of her all-time favorite movies was The Quiet Man. She had spent countless hours as a child imagining she was Maureen O'Hara, stubborn and strong, living in the gorgeous Irish countryside. The movie would be a perfect combination of her Secret Santa person's favorites infused with a small piece of her childhood. She bought the DVD and had it gift-wrapped, attaching a small card that said "Merry Christmas from your Secret Santa #23.

*****

The next day brought no presents from Zoe's Secret Santa. There weren't any rules about when they had to start the gift-giving process, but she was still a little disappointed when the couriers dropped off her ordinary manila envelopes. To make matters worse, she received an email from Logan Baneford asking for further details on job performance for six of her employees. A Secret Santa gift would have done wonders for her drooping spirit.

The following day, however, Zoe was in luck. Almost immediately that morning, she received a long red box, about the size of a box of tapered candles. A card accompanied the box with the number twenty-three scrawled on top. She fought the urge to open the parcel first and carefully freed the card from its envelope.

> *Dear #23,*
>
> *I'm not sure if it was intentional or accidental, but it would seem we ended up drawing each other's numbers. I had considered contacting HR about the mix-up, but then it occurred to me that this may actually be a good thing. Now I won't have to wait until the company Christmas party to thank you for the movie. I haven't seen The Quiet Man in years. My grandmother used to tell me that I should*

find a woman just like Kate. That if a woman didn't challenge me and stand up to me, she wasn't worth marrying. Anyway, thank you for the gift. It has always held a special place in my heart. I hope you enjoy my gift to you. I was pleased to find we have a few similarities, which made the selection process a bit easier.

Sincerely,

#72

Zoe grinned as she ripped into the package and gasped once her gift was freed. Two obnoxiously sparkly drumsticks glittered under her office lights. She twirled them around in her hands and giggled. She was a total nerd in that she loved to play drums on the silly video game, Rock Band, with her nieces and nephews. She had totally forgotten she put that on her questionnaire! She carefully placed them back into their box and vowed to find an even more perfect gift for number seventy-two the next day.

*****

Her next gift was an attempt to combine both of their favorite types of music. While Zoe's tastes were pretty eclectic, she tended to lean toward classic rock and even a bit of heavy metal. Number seventy-two listed out a few classical composers, including Paganini and Tchaikovsky, both of whom wrote scores heavy on the strings sections. Zoe's solution was to purchase a CD by Apocalyptica, a heavy metal band comprised of three exceptionally gifted cellists. She wrapped the CD and delivered it to the couriers' station the next day along with her own note.

Dear #72,

I'm so glad you enjoyed the movie and I'm delighted that we drew one another's number. I'm being completely honest when I say that the drumsticks were one of the best presents I've ever received. I absolutely love them! Thank you!

I hope you like your next gift. Give it a shot! I think it's a perfect mix of both of our styles. You'll have to let me know what you think.

Sincerely,

#23

While Zoe had no doubt that seventy-two would enjoy the CD, she was still overjoyed to read his thank you letter the next day. Of course, he enjoyed it. He admitted to being skeptical but said after the first verse of the first song, he was hooked. And even better, his gift to her was sensational. She had no idea how he'd found it, but nestled in an adorable little ring box sat a tea ball infuser shaped like the Golden Snitch from the Harry Potter series. She hugged the gift to her chest and immediately went on a mission to find her very favorite tea. While it may have seemed ridiculous to anyone else, she could have sworn the tea tasted even better than usual.

And so the Secret Santa Exchange went; each day brought a new gift, a new letter, and a new insight into her friend's life. Zoe spent an outrageous amount of time perfecting her lemon bar recipe to satisfy seventy-two's craving for lemon merengue pie. That gift turned out even better than she had expected, as he informed her the following day in his letter that his mother used to bake him lemon bars. Years before, she was diagnosed with early onset Alzheimer's and had recently passed away. His thank-you letter brought Zoe to tears, and her heart ached for the sweet man.

In return, seventy-two sent her a bag of his "super special secret homemade trail mix." Zoe had mentioned in her questionnaire that she loved the outdoors and chocolate. She laughed way harder than necessary when she saw the note accompanying the bag of chocolate chips and M&Ms.

This is my super special secret homemade trail mix. Guard the recipe with your life. It's been passed down for generations. I did alter it a bit. Nobody cares for the peanuts or raisins, so I left those out. Enjoy!

*****

Before Zoe knew it, it was the night of the company Christmas party. She stood in front of her bathroom mirror and applied her makeup for the fourth time. Her hands were shaking so badly, her eyeliner looked like a seismograph reading. For two weeks she had been exchanging gifts and letters with a stranger. Except that by the end of those two weeks, she felt closer to this man she had never met than she felt toward almost anyone. What if he was married? What if he was old enough to be her grandfather? What if he had halitosis so bad that his breath burned her eyebrows off?

"You've got to chill out." Maisy stood in the doorway observing Zoe's mini mental breakdown. "The guy got you glittery drumsticks and some weird bag of cheap chocolate. That's not exactly love material."

Zoe glanced at Maisy's reflection in the vanity mirror. "I'm not saying it's love," she argued. "I'm just saying it's…I don't know! I've just built him up in my head as this unbelievably amazing, gorgeous, thoughtful, perfect man. What if he's just absolutely dreadful?"

"Then you come home, crack open a bottle of wine and eat that entire bag of chocolate." Maisy stepped forward and smacked Zoe on the behind. "You'll be fine. It's an open bar until nine. Let's just go to the party, have fun with our coworkers and treat the Secret Santa thing like it's just a small piece of a great night."

Zoe forced a smile and took a cleansing breath. "You're right. Let's do this."

*****

The Bane Incorporated lobby was decorated to the nines. For a company about to go through layoffs, they sure did spend a bundle on decor. Zoe filed that information away for future use against Logan and snagged a glass of champagne from the first server she encountered. Maisy was collecting their name badges and the little stickies on which their Secret Santa numbers were displayed. Zoe was on a mission to down enough liquid courage to face her pseudo-fear. By the time her friend returned, she had consumed three glasses of champagne and was searching out a server for her fourth.

"Whoa. Easy, girl!" Maisy popped into Zoe's line of sight and helped pin her name badge on. "I know you're nervous that 'mystery dude' will turn out to be a doorknob, but what if he ends up being amazing and you're too trashed to tell?"

Zoe gasped. "Ugh! You're right!" She buried her face in her hands and groaned. "I can't do this. I can't. I need a stand-in." Her head snapped up. "You! You can be my stand-in!"

Maisy held both hands up and took a step back. "Oh, no. No way, hon. I love you, but I'm not going off to meet the man of your dreams. What if he falls in love with me? I'm adorable! I'm hilarious! And I'll end up stealing your boyfriend and you'll hate me forever because I'll be off on some beach doing dirty things with the love of your life!"

Zoe put on her best puppy dog eyes and poofed her lip out. "Please, Maisy. Please, please? I just can't do it! I promise if he ends up being halfway decent, I'll swoop in and explain that you were only doing me a favor."

Maisy attempted to out-stare the puppy dog look and failed miserably. "Fine. Give me your darn number. You owe me big time!"

Zoe let out a tiny squeal of delight and hugged her friend close. "Thank you! I love you so much! Okay, okay. I'll keep your number in my pocket so you can still use it to find your real Secret Santa. Now go find my seventy-two. I'll be at the bar watching!"

She waited until Maisy disappeared into the crowd before turning and seeking out her destination. After subtly elbowing her way through the crowd, she spotted an empty hightop table situated between the dance floor and the bar. She perched on the accompanying high stool and watched as Maisy worked the crowd, greeting coworkers and scanning number badges.

"Is this seat taken?" A very masculine, very familiar voice broke through Zoe's concentration. Logan Baneford slid onto the stool next to her and handed her a fresh glass of champagne.

"Thank you," Zoe replied, taking a much too large sip. She glanced at his number badge and snorted. "Number one? You drew number one?"

Logan shrugged and took a sip of the dark amber liquid in his glass. "Lucky, I guess."

"Do you at least give good gifts?"

The side of his mouth quirked up into a small smile. "I'd like to think so." He turned on his stool to regard her fully. "Are you enjoying the party?"

She took a sip of her champagne before answering. "It's beautiful. People seem to be having a good time. Decor is top notch."

Logan sighed and set his drink down. "How can I fix this?"

Zoe shook her head in confusion. "Fix what?"

He motioned between the two of them with his hand. "This. Us. How can I fix our working relationship so I don't feel ice crystals on my eyebrows after we have a conversation?"

Zoe bit her lip and fiddled with her napkin. "I don't know," she answered honestly. "It's hard to be here at this extravagant party that cost you an obscene amount of money when I know you're about to lay off members of my work family. And even worse, you talk about it as if it means nothing to you."

Logan reached out a hand and placed it over Zoe's, giving her a light squeeze. "Zoe, I don't think you understand how much I hate laying people off. I hate it. But I can't pay multiple people to perform the same tasks every day. I've spent these past couple of weeks going through job descriptions, attempting to shift responsibilities and cut down on the number of job cuts by as much as possible. Two weeks ago we were looking at letting four hundred people go. This morning we recounted and we're down to thirty. And every one of those thirty people have had extremely sub-par reviews for multiple years. Even then, we're giving them three months of severance pay and I've contacted several business associates in the city who are hiring. Those thirty people will not be jobless for long if I can help it."

Zoe sat frozen on her stool, dumbfounded by what Logan was telling her. The man she'd been trying so hard to dislike had officially made it darn near impossible to not admire him.

"Wow!" She sighed. "I feel like such a jerk."

Logan offered a small smile and shrugged. "Look, I get it. I didn't really want to take on this role anyway. I'm not sure if you were aware, but Marvin Sumner wasn't ready to retire. His health has seriously deteriorated over the past couple of years. He's a family friend and he basically begged me to take over his company. Obviously, I wouldn't have purchased the business if it weren't a financially sound decision. But I hate being the bad guy and I knew I would be."

"You're not the bad guy," Zoe disagreed. "You're the misunderstood guy."

"Oh. My. God." Maisy rushed toward the table. "I need to talk to you. Right now." She cast a pointed look at Logan.

"Um…I'll just be over there." Logan turned back to Zoe and smiled. "I'll talk to you later?"

She nodded and tried not to notice his bum as he walked away.

"Hello! Earth to space cadet!" Maisy waved her hands in front of Zoe's face.

"What? What happened?"

"I found number seventy-two! And Zoe…I'm so sorry, hon. You know that guy in IT whose tighty-whiteys stick out of his pants?"

Zoe gasped. "The one who only uses pens shaped like light sabers?"

"Yes!" Maisy nodded. "It's him! And I thought that maybe he was actually really smooth and the exterior was just a bit rough. So I asked him if he'd like to dance. He smells like cat urine and spent the entire time talking about how his mother hadn't washed his favorite Yoda socks for the party."

"I'm gonna need more champagne." Zoe drained what was left in her glass.

"I'm so sorry." Maisy rubbed a comforting hand down Zoe's back.

"I should've known," Zoe groaned as she returned Maisy's real number badge. "Nobody's that perfect. I shouldn't have let myself get sucked into the Hollywood love story crap."

"Screw the champagne," Maisy proclaimed as she pinned the badge on her dress. "We need tequila."

"Tequila?" Logan reappeared from behind Zoe with two glasses of champagne in hand. "Hitting the hard stuff so soon?"

Zoe grabbed both champagne glasses from him and downed them, coughing slightly as the bubbles raced up and through her nose.

"Yikes," Logan murmured. He arched an eyebrow at Maisy. "I'm guessing you didn't come with good news."

She shook her head solemnly and gave Zoe's shoulder another pat. "Let's just say she's having a mistletoe meltdown."

Logan smiled through his obvious confusion before glancing at Maisy's number badge. "Number thirty-one. Just who I've been looking for."

"You're number one?" Maisy leaned forward as if to inspect the authenticity of Logan's badge. At his confirming nod, she smiled politely. "Thank you for the gifts. The chocolate Christmas trees were delicious."

"Chocolate Christmas trees?" Zoe scoffed, emboldened by her many glasses of champagne. "I thought you said you gave good gifts?"

Logan attempted to look offended, but his grin broke through. "I happen to love chocolate Christmas trees. I read that my Secret Santa recipient loved chocolate. It's the Christmas season. I combined the two. Boom. Chocolate Christmas trees." He mimicked Zoe's exaggerated eye roll and nudged her with his elbow. "At least I picked it out myself instead of having my assistant go out to purchase the gifts."

"I'll tell you what," Maisy offered. "I'll let you buy us some tequila shots to make up for your lame gifts."

Logan laughed and placed an arm around each of the ladies' shoulders. "Deal. Let's go toast to lame gifts, mistletoe meltdowns and awkward company Christmas parties."

*****

The following Monday evening, Zoe sat at her computer answering emails and trying desperately to ignore the little Golden Snitch tea ball sitting abandoned on her desk. She was about to log off for the day when a new email appeared in her Inbox. It was from Logan Baneford.

> Zoe,
>
> *I just wanted to send you a quick note to let you know that the "thirty" we discussed last Friday has been cut down to twenty-five. And none of those twenty-five are on your team. You did a wonderful job hiring great employees and it definitely shows.*
>
> Have a good week.
>
> Logan

Zoe glanced at the clock. It was after six o'clock but he had just sent the email. Hoping to catch him before he left, she quickly shut down her computer and rushed to his office. He was just buttoning his overcoat when she bustled through the door.

"Zoe! What a nice surprise." He smiled warmly and motioned for her to sit.

"I just wanted to thank you for your email and to apologize again for my attitude."

"I appreciate it," he replied. "But it's not necessary. I would have felt the same way." His eyes landed on her shoulder and caught on something. "You've got some glitter there."

Zoe glanced down and grinned at the little sparkle. "I keep finding them everywhere. My Secret Santa gave me these hilarious glittery drumsticks."

Logan froze. "What?"

"I know it sounds silly, but they were really spectacular." Zoe giggled and shook her head at the memory. "I wrote on my questionnaire that I love to play the drums in Rock Band. It was actually really sweet of him."

Logan remained still with a very peculiar look on his face. "Twenty-three?"

Zoe's laughter quickly halted as she stared back at him. "How do you know my number?"

"How can you be twenty-three? I was told she was a platinum blonde, uber-obnoxious woman from Accounting."

"I switched numbers with a friend," Zoe answered. "Why were you asking about twenty-three?"

Logan burst into laughter. "Let me guess, your friend told you that number seventy-two was a socially awkward Star Wars fan from IT?"

Zoe's heart lurched. "You didn't switch numbers, too…Did you?"

Logan nodded and stepped closer. "I realize I'm a full-grown man, but I kind of chickened out."

A smile spread across Zoe's lips as she absorbed the shock. "I think I secretly hoped it was you," she whispered.

Logan closed the remaining distance between them and cupped her cheek in his palm. "What won you over? The super special trail mix?"

Zoe stood on her tip toes and lightly pressed her lips against his. "Duh. Chocolate is always the best way to a woman's heart. And sparkly drumsticks, of course."

CHRISTMAS LIGHTS
BY
P.J. HICK

"It's about time you got here."

Detective Ripley Brown stared at the gentleman in the doorway of the stately brick two-story house. He was a little man with a big bald spot on the top of his head, and he wore wire-rimmed glasses. He was dressed in a plaid flannel shirt and a pair of dark blue jeans. Brown guessed his age to be about fifty.

"Why is that, Mr. Dickens?" Brown asked.

The other man wrung his hands in desperation. "This just can't go on. The judging of the Christmas lights is tomorrow and if the thief keeps this up, I'm bound to lose."

Brown wrinkled his brow. "What?"

"The thief keeps taking my light bulbs. Here I'll show you." Dickens put on his winter coat and led the detective into the yard in front of his house. He pointed to a bush draped with cords and lights. "He took six of these light bulbs. With so many missing, the whole string won't come on. The day before, he took four lights from Frosty the Snowman, and before that seven from Rudolph's nose."

"I see," Detective Brown said.

"It's been happening all week. I go to work and by the time I get home, something is missing. I need you to put an end to this." Dickens crossed his arms in front of his chest and stomped his foot.

"How many lights do you have on your house?"

"Thirty-seven thousand."

Detective Brown blinked his eyes. "Thirty-seven thousand, you say."

"Yes. It's taken my family a month to put them all up. The whole house is outlined with them twice. The outline changes colors, from red to green every ten seconds." Dickens waved his hand as he talked. "Frosty over there tips his hat to the audience, and the reindeers' legs move. Santa Claus waves and Merry Christmas is spelled out along that side of the roof. It's taken me years to perfect the system and I won't have someone ruining my display for their own selfish gain. I have to defend my title, after all. I've won the Chamber of Commerce Best Individual House award three years in a row. And I will win it again, in spite of them."

"Who's them?"

"The other residents in the city, of course. Why, it wouldn't surprise me if Sam Nicholas who lives up the street is behind it all. He didn't even put up lights this year, which cost me and the other people on this block the best street award. What a Grinch."

For the next half hour, Detective Brown listened patiently to Mr. Dickens' complaints. He tried hard not to show his annoyance at the whole situation. In his opinion, the holiday season brought out the worst in people. Shoplifting, robberies and burglaries increased. The good old family get-togethers resulted in domestic abuse and assaults. Other people drank too much and then decided to drive, usually resulting in death or severe injuries.

Somehow, Brown couldn't get too excited about a few stolen Christmas lights, especially since it was obvious that Mr. Dickens was affluent to start with and could afford to replace some missing light bulbs.

But it was his responsibility to investigate the matter and Detective Brown wasn't about to shirk his duty. He knew the patrol officers were fed up with Mr. Dickens' phone calls. That's why the police department had sent a detective out this time, to calm the man down. Patrol had increased their surveillance of the area, but had not discovered the person doing the vandalism. There was little evidence to go on, and it had snowed two inches earlier in the day, erasing any of the villain's tracks.

After leaving Mr. Dickens' property, Brown strolled to the house next door and rang the bell. It too was decorated with lights for the holidays. A petite, middle-aged blond woman adorned in expensive clothes and heavy makeup answered the door.

"Hi, I'm Detective Brown." He showed his badge to the woman. "I'm investigating the theft of some Christmas lights at Mr. Dickens' residence and I was wondering if I could ask you a few questions?"

The woman rolled her eyes in their sockets. "That man is obsessed with his Christmas lights. He can't stand to lose his freaking award. Ever since he moved over there, he has pestered his neighbors to put up lights. It's become a sin if you don't. Just look up and down the street. Everyone does it. The first year I thought it was kind of fun. Now I couldn't care less."

"Ah, have you lost any lights, Mrs...."

"Kane. Candace Kane." She nodded her head. "A few. The fact is I wish they would have taken them all. Every darn one of them. Maybe then we could live in peace around here."

"Ah, have you seen anyone out of the ordinary in your neighborhood? You know, someone that doesn't live around here?"

The woman laughed. A big booming laugh that ricocheted off the door she was holding open and out into the air. She gasped for air and then laughed again, her chest heaving with the effort.

"What's so funny?" Detective Brown wrinkled his forehead in puzzlement.

"I'm sorry..." The woman could barely get the words out as she almost choked on her laughter. It took several minutes for her to get control of herself. By then tears were falling from her eyes. She wiped them away with her free hand.

"I can see, Detective, that you have never lived next to a national spectacle. I believe everyone in the city and maybe the entire state has driven down this street at night during the month of December. Television cameras appear. News reporters pound on doors to get interviews. Business and charity organizations plan bus trips to tour our neighborhood. I've seen about every kind of idiot you can imagine. There are days when I feel like an animal in a zoo."

Brown smiled.

"Come back after the sun goes down, and you'll see what I mean. I'm just thankful we don't live in Alaska, then we'd have a traffic jam in front of our houses all day long."

"I think I get the picture."

"I bet you do."

The detective tried a few more houses, with similar responses from the people he found at home. It was late afternoon when he reached Sam Nicholas' home.

The winter day had turned nasty and the temperature had dropped a couple degrees in the last hour. A gust of wind stung Brown's cheek.

"Cold isn't it, officer?" a stout old man in a worn tan coat said, as he stopped shoveling the snow in his driveway. The man had big, insulated gloves on and a red stocking hat that fitted snugly over his ears.

"Yes it is. I take it you must be Mr. Nicholas," Detective Brown said, as he surveyed the man.

"That's me," Nicholas replied. "And you're trying to find out who stole Dickens' Christmas lights, I reckon?"

Detective Brown's head slightly tipped to the side and one eyebrow rose. "How did you know?"

"Doesn't take much to figure out something as simple as that, now does it, sonny? And as for your other question, no I'm not the responsible party, even though Dickens has accused me of it, time and time again."

"He has?"

The old man leaned heavily on the handle of his snow shovel. "Sure. Every time it's happened. Just this morning he telephoned and threatened to have me arrested. And now here you are."

The old man's blue eyes gleamed with a twinkle of hidden knowledge and wisdom as he leaned a little closer to the detective. "You aren't going to arrest me, now are you young man?"

"No," Detective Brown replied. "But I would like to know why you didn't put up any lights this year."

The old man straightened up and snorted through his nose. "Christmas is a time to bring happiness to others, and not for feuding and back-biting. I refuse to surrender the true spirit of the season to that greedy, egotistical cynic. I have better things to do than play his game. All he wants is his name on the front page and his image in front of a crowd."

"How do you know that?"

"At night he parades outside his house and waves to the buses going past. He hopes someone will leap out and take a photograph of him. Most of the time somebody does."

Nicholas stuck his nose in the air, puffed his chest up, and strutted around his shovel in a circle, mimicking the action as he spoke. "I've never seen anything like it. It's enough to make a person puke. Trust me, whoever is taking those light bulbs should get a medal of honor."

Detective Brown could only nod in response. This case was turning out to be anything but easy. It appeared Mr. Dickens had enough enemies in his neighborhood to start World War III. As far as Brown was concerned, everybody he had talked to this afternoon was a suspect.

Detective Brown walked back to his unmarked police car, pondering what to do next. He could stake out Dickens' house or put a video camera on it. He was surprised Dickens hadn't thought of that himself. Yet it seemed overkill for a bunch of light bulbs.

Sliding into his car, he started the engine and flipped on the heater, glancing once more around the neighborhood, his eyes looking up and down the street. He noted the fresh tracks that he and Dickens had made on his lawn, and reviewed in his head the locations where all the stolen light bulbs had been taken. They had all been within easy reach, no higher than his own waist level.

His gaze came to rest on a small boy walking up the sidewalk, a plastic sled rolled up underneath his arm. There was nothing extraordinary about the boy, but something drew his attention back to the figure. The boy wore an oversized coat, a knit hat and big black rubber boots. Brown guessed him to be about nine years old.

The boy turned his head and looked warily at the car. He caught Brown looking at him and increased his pace to a fast walk.

Brown shifted his car into gear and drove slowly up the street. When he was even with the boy, he rolled down his window. "I'm Detective Brown." He held up his badge. "Can I talk to you a minute, son?"

The boy's big brown eyes widened in surprise in his dark face as he stopped walking. "Yes, sir."

"What's your name?"

"Tyrone Richardson." the boy said, clutching his sled tightly and balancing back and forth on his feet.

"Do you live around here, Tyrone?"

"I live on East 10th Street."

"That's kind of far away, isn't it?"

The boy licked his lips. "I'm going to the park to play. I'm meeting friends there."

"You play there often?"

"Uh-hum."

"You haven't seen anybody taking Christmas tree lights in this neighborhood have you?" He barely got the words out when the boy bolted down the street at a full run. Brown followed him in the car. "Hey, wait!"

The boy darted across a lawn of a beige house away from the officer. He ran flat out and almost disappeared from sight behind it by the time Detective Brown turned his car off and leaped out after the boy.

"Damn," Ripley cussed, as he chased the youngster. It was obvious the boy knew where he was going. The kid raced through two backyards and crossed the street into Beaver Park. Brown was gaining on him with every stride. "Stop! Police!"

The boy looked back at the detective and moved into yet a higher gear and ran on. He twisted his way around the frozen pond, swing set, the jungle gym, and ran toward the sledding hill. When Brown was within a couple strides of the boy, the youngster spread out his plastic sled and hurled his body onto it with youthful abandon. The sled and boy slid away at blazing speed down the park's steep hill.

Brown tried to halt his momentum, but it was no use. He fought to keep his balance on the icy surface of the hill, staying upright for a moment before his feet flew out from under him. He landed hard on his butt and back and began to roll sideways down the slope, stopping with a thud at the base. When he looked up, and he saw a tiny figure running half way across the bottom of the park to disappear behind some trees. He groaned as he got to his feet and knew he'd have bruises tomorrow. As he dusted the snow off his pants, he also dusted off his pride. He was thirty-five years old and in the prime of his life. It disturbed him that he had let a nine-year-old kid get the better of him.

Wait a minute. Maybe... he could still salvage this situation. He walked back to his car and called the station. He asked the dispatcher to find a Richardson on East 10th Street. His luck held. The boy had given him a correct address.

The place turned out to be a small ranch house in an older neighborhood. The house, built around the time of WWII, had seen better days. Paint was peeling off its sides, one of the windows was cracked and the pouch sagged.

Detective Brown walked up the wooden steps and knocked on the rusting metal door. A tiny black woman in her early thirties answered. Brown held up his badge.

"Detective Brown, ma'am."

She looked worried when she saw him standing there. "Can I help you, Officer?"

"Does a Tyrone Richardson live here?"

"He does. What's this about?" The woman's hands began to shake. But before Brown could answer, she added, "My son is a good boy. He doesn't run with any gangs. He gets straight A's in school and he goes to church. He knows I would skin him alive if he got into any trouble."

"Ah, yes. I'm not accusing him of anything. But there are some Christmas lights missing on some houses on Grand Avenue, and since he was walking around in that neighborhood, I thought he might have seen something. But he ran away before he would answer me."

"Christmas lights? That's it? Just some Christmas lights!" The woman turned and hollered into the room. "Tyrone. Come here, please."

Tyrone appeared and looked sheepishly at his mother and the detective.

With her arms crossed over her chest, his mother asked, "Do you know anything about missing Christmas lights?"

Tyrone hung his head and looked at the floor.

"Tyrone, I asked you a question?"

Slowly, he raised his head and looked Detective Brown in the eye. "Are you going to put me in jail?"

"Depends," Detective Brown said.

"On what?"

"Whether or not you tell the truth."

Tyrone's lip began to quiver as he glanced at his mamma, then back at the Detective. He nodded his head. "I took 'em."

Brown saw the mother's eyes widen in surprise. She reached out her hand and gently shook her son's shoulder. "Why did you do that? You know better."

His face etched in sorrow, Tyrone looked at his mother. "Because, Dad always put up the lights. But he's dead, and I had no money. So I took 'em. I wanted to do it for you, Mamma. As a Christmas present because you've been so sad."

The woman turned to face the detective. He could see that her eyes were clouded with tears. He felt her discomfort and didn't know what to do with the feeling.

Clearing her throat, she whispered, "Detective, how much trouble is my boy in?"

Brown looked at the woman and then at the boy. "I think if he returns the lights, I can make the owner drop the charges."

"Tyrone, go get the lights." the woman said sadly.

The boy bolted out of the room as if he was shot out of a cannon. In a few minutes he reappeared with a sack overflowing with light bulbs. He offered the bag to Detective Brown.

"Go get your coat on." The woman nudged her son toward the living room closet. "You owe some people an apology. And you're going with the Detective to return those lights."

Tyrone followed the detective out to his car and got inside. They didn't talk as they took the short drive from the boy's home to the plush part of town.

It took much longer to convince Mr. Dickens not to press charges. The man bellowed and shook his fist as he raged on about the decaying morals of today's youth. But in the end he agreed to be satisfied with the return of his property.

Mrs. Kane next door was easier to convince.

The sun had begun to set when Detective Brown parked his car once again in the driveway of the small house on E. 10th Street. Brown looked at the dejected boy huddled as far away as he could get in the corner of the front seat of his car. He looked small and pitiful. As the boy pulled the latch to open the door, Brown said, "You won't steal anything else will you, Tyrone?"

The boy shook his head. "No sir. Never again." He climbed out of the car, then stopped and looked directly at the detective. "But it ain't right that they should have all the lights and we have none. It's dark here." He waved his hand toward the street where not a single house had Christmas lights. With that he slammed the door and walked with his shoulders sagging toward the house.

Brown watched the boy go until he disappeared into the house. For the rest of the shift, his mind wondered back to Tyrone. The whole light bulb incident bothered him. He thought about it the rest of the night.

He thought about it again the next morning over his coffee and later when he worked out at the gym. He thought about it as he finished his Christmas shopping in the malls glistening with seasonal decorations. The cheerfulness of the window displays only added to his gloom. It was his day off and he should be enjoying himself, but he wasn't. All he could see was one small boy with a hurt inside as big a football field.

He had to do something. Detective Brown went to a hardware store and bought as many strings of Christmas lights as he could find. He didn't know how to put them up, but he figured he could learn.

When he reached Tyrone's house, he found he was too late. Other elves had beaten him there. Perched high on a ladder was Sam Nicholas, and assisting him from the ground was Candace Kane. Tyrone stood beside her, directing their activities with his small hands and a smile as wide as the planet Jupiter on his face.

Brown approached the group. "Could you use some more lights?"

Sam nodded, and together the three of them strung them along the roof of the house. Mrs. Richardson, not to be outdone by their generosity, came out with Christmas cookies and hot chocolate as a reward for their labor.

When dusk came, Tyrone flipped the electricity on and all the adults stared at their handiwork. Golden lights outlined the sides of the humble dwelling. High above the porch in the center of the roof, the silhouette of a bright silver star twinkled on and off like a beacon in the night.

Tyrone's mother, who was standing next to Detective Brown, gasped in wonderment. Brown too, was taken aback by the simple display. No star in Bethlehem could have shone as bright.

"Now that's what I call a Christmas light," Sam Nicholas said.

"You know, Sam, I couldn't agree with you more."

A Christmas Miracle
By
Magnolia "Maggie" Rivers

Clarissa McKnight stared at the man standing on her front porch.

"What the hell?" she exclaimed.

"Excuse me?" he said.

"Excuse you to hell and back. What the hell are you doing showing up on my doorstep after fifteen years?"

"Excuse me, Miss…um," Chad flipped through his notepad and found the name, "if this is the McKnight residence, I'm supposed to be meeting a Clarissa McKnight about building a gazebo."

"Well, John, you were supposed to meet Clarissa McKnight at the airport fifteen years ago to get married. You're a little late." Tears played at the corners of Clarissa's eyes.

"Miss, I'm sorry, but you must have me mixed up with someone else. I'm Chad Williams. I'm here from Williams Construction."

Clarissa stared at the man in front of her. Chad was not the name she knew. He was John Connor. Same green eyes, same sandy brown hair and the same childhood scar above his left eye. She knew that scar. He was taller and more muscular than when she had last seen him. Her pulse raced at the sight of him. It always had. Her fingers itched to play across his chest as they had so many times when she was eighteen.

"They told me you were discharged once you got back to the mainland. You never even called me."

"Miss, I'm sorry. You obviously think you know me but I don't know you. I'm Chad Williams. I own Williams Construction. I live in Tuscaloosa. Across the river there. Moved here three years ago."

"Chad, huh?" Clarissa stood looking at the man. This was John. Her John. They had lived next door to each other since she was two. He'd been her protector, her soulmate. At least until he joined the Air Force. He had asked her to wait for him. He would marry her if he made it back. She'd wanted to marry before he left for Afghanistan but he'd said no. He didn't want to leave a widow behind.

When his time was up, she flew out to meet him. But, it had snowed and her plane was delayed for two hours. When her plane finally touched down he was gone. Until this moment.

"Well, Chad Williams, I don't know what game you're playing but it's not funny to me. That scar above your eye, I put it there when you were seven. And the gash on the calf of your right leg is from a bicycle accident. I was there for that, too. So, you can call yourself by any name you want, but I know who you are. Now, get off my property. I don't want to see you ever again."

"Whatever you say, lady," said Chad as he closed his notebook, stepped off the porch and headed back to his truck.

"Crazy woman," Chad whispered under his breath. Too bad, too. She was cute.

Clarissa let the screen snap shut as she slammed the wooden door inside and leaned against it. Her body shook uncontrollably as she slid down onto the floor. Her breath came in ragged gasps.

Well, Merry Christmas to me!

Hot tears burned her cheeks as heavy sobs racked her body.

*****

"Sweetie, are you okay?" asked Jane when she caught the look on Clarissa's face as she opened the door.

"No," replied Clarissa, "I'm not sure I'll ever be okay. John showed up on my doorstep and tried to convince me he was someone else."

"John. Oh my God!" said Jane. "After what, fifteen years, he just shows up? What did he want?"

"He was the builder Matt sent out to give me an estimate on building a gazebo out back."

"Matt knows him?"

"No, no. Matt called a construction company and John shows up."

"Well butter my butt and call me a biscuit," said Jane as she steered Clarissa back into the living room. "So, let me get this straight. John shows up and tells you he's somebody else and he's here to build a gazebo for you."

"Something like that."

"Are you sure it was him?"

"Yeah. Same eyes, same hair, same scar above his eyebrow. I put that scar there. I know it was John. And I'm sure if I could have seen his leg, that scar would be there, too."

"Oh my goodness, what'd he do?"

"Nothing. He kept telling me he was Chad Williams."

"He just shows up out of the blue like that. If that don't beat all. Did he say where he'd been all this time?"

"No, he kept trying to convince me he was this Chad guy."

"So what are you going to do now?"

"Do? I'm not doing anything. Matt and I are getting married tomorrow remember and then we're spending Christmas in Hawaii."

"Good for you, if that's what you want."

"What do you mean 'if that's what I want?'" Clarissa stared at Jane.

"Well, I think John at least owes you an explanation. I mean, you flew all the way out there to meet him. You couldn't help it because the weather didn't cooperate. I mean, I'm sure they told him why the plane was delayed. He knew you were on that plane. He didn't wait. Why? Why didn't he wait? I'd want to know."

"It took me years to get over it but I'm over it. I'm over him. His loss, not mine."

"I know, sweetie, it is definitely his loss. The jerk. I just think he owes you an explanation."

"Well, I don't want to hear his excuse. I'm better off without him. Besides, that chapter of my life is over anyway. I'm marrying Matt this weekend, so it's a moot point."

"Sweetheart, can I ask you something really personal?"

"Oh, Jane, you know you can ask me anything."

"Have you really moved on?"

"Moved on?"

"I mean are you sure you're really in love with Matt?"

"Of course I am. Matt is a wonderful person. He just fits. He's comfortable, you know. We'll be happy together."

"Comfortable."

"Yes, Matt is comfortable. He may not make rockets explode but he's good to me. He takes care of me. Maybe when you've been deserted at the altar you're a little more careful about who you choose next time. Matt is very dependable. We'll be happy together."

"Sweetie, did you listen to yourself? I mean really listen."

"What? What'd I say?"

"It's not what you said, hon, it's what you didn't say."

"What is it? What are you trying to say?"

"Nowhere in all that talk about Matt did you say you loved him."

"Well, of course, I love Matt."

"Well, as long as you're not still in love with John."

"It'll be a cold day in hell when I have any feelings for John Connor. He's out of my life for good." At least he had been. Why in the world did he have to show up today? She was better off without him.

"Okay, then. Go fix your makeup and let's go to the Café and have dinner. You need a change of scenery," said Jane as she stood up from the couch and pulled Clarissa up with her. "Now scoot," she continued as she turned Clarissa in the direction of her bedroom.

*****

Walking into the Market Café, Clarissa and Jane found a table toward the back.

"Hey girls, be right with ya," yelled Nadine as she set glasses of iced tea down on the table behind them.

"What looks good to you, Claire?" asked Jane as she perused her menu.

"I'm going for the cheeseburger and fries," replied Clarissa as she closed the menu, un-folded her napkin and laid it across her lap.

"Sounds good to me, too," said Jane as Nadine walked up beside them.

"So what brings you two ladies out and about this evening?" asked Nadine as she took her pen and notepad from her apron pocket.

"I think it was the cheeseburger calling," said Clarissa as she laughed.

"I hear ya," replied Nadine, "one cheeseburger and you want fries, too?"

"What's a cheeseburger without fries?" asked Jane.

"I hear ya, girl. I'll make that two cheeseburgers with fries and sweet iced tea."

"Thanks, Nadine. How's Billy these days?" asked Clarissa.

"Oh he's fine as frog's hair," said Nadine as she headed back towards the kitchen.

"My Lord!" exclaimed Jane.

"What?" Clarissa asked as she turned to see what Jane was staring at.

"My Lord! That is John," gasped Jane.

"Why in the world would he show up here?" asked Clarissa.

"Probably to eat," said Jane. "I mean it is a café."

"Oh hell, wait a minute. I'll be right back," said Clarissa as she pulled a wedding invitation from her purse, got up and walked over to John who was still standing at the front of the café waiting for a seat.

"Well, let's see, it's Chad isn't it. Well, Chad, just so you know," she said as she stuffed the wedding invitation into his shirt pocket, "I'm getting married this weekend. Feel free to come and watch how a real man does it." She slapped his shirt pocket against his chest, turned and walked back to her table.

Chad watched the woman. She was intriguing to say the least, and…there was something familiar about the sway of her hips. But he was positive he had never seen her before. The face of a laughing young girl sped through his mind.

Damn it. What the hell!

"Grab a seat any place," yelled Nadine as she hurried out of the back carrying plates of food.

He took a seat in the front corner of the café and picked up the menu from its holder on the table. Nadine hustled by, taking his order. It wasn't long before she was back placing today's special on the table in front of him.

"Enjoy, hon," she said, "and yell if you need something."

Moments later, he watched the two women get up from their table and walk out the front door, which was too bad as he was definitely enjoying the view.

"Can I get you anything else, Chad, honey?" asked Nadine.

"I'm just fine, Nadine. I'm full as a tick sittin' on an artery."

"Well, that has to be pretty darn full." She laughed.

Chad stood up from the table and dropped a tip before sticking his wallet back into this pocket.

"I'll be back tomorrow night for some more of your good home cookin'."

"I'll be sure to save you a piece of apple pie then."

"You definitely know the way to a man's heart." Chad laughed. "You tell that man of yours, he better be treatin' you real good or I'm gonna steal you away."

"Oh, go on with ya bad self now," said Nadine as she turned and headed back toward the kitchen.

Chad opened the door and walked outside in the fresh night air. He stood looking up at the moon for a moment. Laughter stirred something in his mind. The moon, a river bank and that beautiful laughter. Chad rested his hand against the brick wall of the building as he stopped to let his senses clear.

He didn't understand all these bits and pieces of things he saw in his mind or the things he heard. PTSD the doc had said but Chad had a feeling it was something else entirely. He'd had his first one the day he stopped for gas at a station up the road. He'd been on his way moving to Miami. There was something about Tuscaloosa. It felt so familiar. Then he saw that big ol' yellow moon winking at him and he'd pulled into the parking lot of the motel. That had been the first time his mind had conjured the image of the laughing girl.

It had to have been the moon that started it this time. Once his head cleared, he turned and headed down the sidewalk and turned the corner toward the parking lot in back.

*****

"Chad, Chad, honey, don't move," said Nadine as she knelt down beside Chad's half unconscious body. "The ambulance is on its way."

Chad opened his eyes and focused on the woman bending over him. He felt strange as bits and pieces of memory raced through his mind. There were conflicting images he didn't understand.

Where was he and who was this woman and why was she calling him Chad? He knew his name. Where was Claire? She was supposed to meet him. No, he remembered her plane had been delayed due to the snow. Something was dreadfully wrong. Something he couldn't quite understand.

"You lie still now. You've been hurt. I don't think anything's broken but you have a nasty lump on your head. Do you remember what happened?" Nadine asked.

"No, no, I don't. I was on my way to meet my fiancée. That's the last thing I remember."

"Your fiancée? Chad, honey, you don't have a fiancée as far as I know. I mean, I've known you now for about three years and you've never mentioned a fiancée."

"Her plane was delayed due to the snow," he replied.

"Chad, honey, it hasn't snowed here in years."

"Why do you keep calling me Chad? My name is John."

"Oh Lord, honey, you just lie still. We'll get you to the hospital and they'll help you straighten this out."

John heard the ambulance pull to a stop and after the EMTs had stabilized him to a board, they lifted him onto the gurney and loaded him in the ambulance.

*****

Dr. William Mason sat at the desk in his psych ward office. He'd been treating patients here for the last forty years and this was the first case he'd seen of this nature.

"Tell me again, John, what you remember?"

"I don't know what it is I'm supposed to remember, Doc. I just got back from Afghanistan, got my discharge papers and was headed to meet my girl. Next thing I know, I'm locked up here in the loony bin talking to a shrink."

"Can you tell me about the years in between meeting your girl at the airport and being here today?"

"Years? What do you mean, years?"

"John, according to your discharge papers you were discharged from the Air Force fifteen years ago."

Dr. Mason watched as the color drained from John's face.

"What the hell?"

"John, I suspect something happened once you got off the plane. Something you saw, felt or heard maybe. Whatever it was, it was bad enough your mind couldn't assimilate it and it chose to protect you the best way it could. Can you understand that?"

"So, you're telling me this, whatever it was, just happened and I decided to check out for fifteen years?"

"Something like that." Dr. Mason watched his patient trying to grasp what he'd been told. "PTSD manifests itself in a variety of ways."

"Then where have I been for the last fifteen years?"

"That's something you may never know, John. I believe you experienced fugue amnesia. Let me see if I can explain it to you."

"Be my guest, Doc."

"You ever hear about people who go out to get a pack of cigarettes or beer or something and they never come back. Sometimes they may be gone for days, other times it's years and sometimes they never come back."

"Like in the movies?"

"Yes, I believe there's been a movie or two about it."

"So, you're saying I got off the plane and walked out of my life."

"Yes. From what we can gather that's what's happened to you. You've had fugue amnesia. Now, your past memories are coming back and whoever you were during those other years has disappeared."

"Well, I'll be damned." John got up out of the chair and walked over to the window.

"What we do know, John, because of the people around here who know you, is you were using the name Chad Williams and you work for Williams Construction. You've lived here in Tuscaloosa for about the last three years. The lady who found you and got you to the hospital was Nadine Johnson and she works at the Market Café there in Northport. She may be able to help fill in some of the pieces."

"So what do I do now?"

"Well, bits and pieces of your life as Chad Williams may come back to you over time. Those years may eventually get filled in. What I want you to watch for now are symptoms of depression. You might even feel guilt or even suicidal tendencies. I want you to watch for any change in your personality. That lump on your head is probably going to give you a headache for a day or two but I'm going to sign off on your discharge. So as soon as Dr. Peters releases you you'll be free to go. I want you to call my office and make an appointment for me to see you again next week. And if you need to see me before then, just call."

"Thanks, Doc, I think." John offered his right hand to Dr. Mason as he combed the fingers of his left hand through his hair.

"Fifteen years ago? Where the hell have I been for fifteen years?"

*****

It was a good thing Nadine had given the hospital admissions his home address since he didn't remember it. He'd checked out of the hospital, hailed a cab and gone there. Miss Betty was glad to see him. It was weird how he remembered her but not the house. He felt strange even to himself.

His head hurt, so after supper he'd gone to his room and turned in for the night, hoping for a better day in the morning.

He'd been dreaming, or at least he thought it was a dream. The laughing girl was back, bringing a flood of memories with her. Clarissa. His Claire. She'd been there in his memories all along. His mind kept trying to find its way back to her.

Now, he had to find her. Where was she? What had happened to her in the last fifteen years? Had she married someone else when he didn't show up? What must she have gone through? They were to be married. Damn it, he had just disappeared, leaving her with no explanation.

He would find her. He at least owed her an explanation.

Morning came way too early. It was nine o'clock when John pushed himself out of bed and stood in the shower letting the hot water relax his tense muscles. Finally, he dried himself off and slipped into his shirt and trousers. He'd already tucked the shirt in before noticing there was something in the pocket. Reaching in, he pulled out the card and read it.

"Claire," he whispered. He quickly looked around the room and found the clock on the wall. It was nine thirty already.

This was not going to be easy but he had to get to the church before it was too late.

*****

Jumping out of Miss Betty's sedan, he ran into the Market Café. It was full on a Saturday morning.

He glanced around and spotted an older lady in a waitress uniform.

"Are you Nadine?" he asked.

"Yes, Chad, how are you feeling? Should you be up?"

"Yeah, I'm okay. Doc released me. Listen, I don't have time to talk. Come with me," he said and grabbed her by the arm, pulling her with him as he headed back outside.

"Honey, what are you doing? Turn me loose," demanded Nadine.

"Can't. You gotta help me get to the church," he said as he reached into his shirt pocket and thrust the wedding invitation at her. "I'll explain on the way. This is Saturday, right?"

"Yeah. Ohhhh, we're heading to a wedding, right?"

"Do you know where this church is?" he asked as he shoved her into Miss Betty's sedan.

"Yeah, it's a few blocks over."

"Good. Get me there? I need to stop a wedding."

"Oh my Lord, put the pedal to the metal then and floor this thing," said Nadine as she grabbed what she called the "Oh Shit" handle in at the top of the truck's door.

*****

Clarissa stood in the church dressing room. Her nerves were on edge. She'd tried to sleep last night but had tossed and turned. Thoughts of John had filled her dreams.

Finally, she had gotten up and made herself a cup of chamomile tea. She knew she had made the right decision. It was just unsettling for John to show up in town now. She'd spent years getting over him and now he shows up right before her Christmas wedding.

She was marrying Matt Brown in a few minutes. It was John's loss, not hers.

"How you holding up?" asked Jane as she stuck her head through the doorway.

"I wish this would hurry up and be over."

"Oh, honey, you don't have to do this if you're having second thoughts," said Jane as she closed the door behind her.

"It's not that. I guess I'm just nervous."

"Every bride gets nervous on her wedding day. You look beautiful, sweetie."

"You think so?"

"Yes, I do. Now, it's about thirty minutes until the music starts and we get this show on the road. Can I get you anything?"

"I could really use a glass of water. My mouth is so dry."

"I'll be right back with one glass of water. You stay put and don't you worry about a thing," said Jane as she quickly slipped back out the doorway and headed to the kitchen in the basement of the church.

*****

"Okay, Nadine, let's go find her," said John as they scurried into the church vestibule.

"Piece of cake," said Nadine. "I'll take this side and you take that one."

A minute later, John caught a glimpse of Nadine waving at him from across the way.

"Come on, she's down that way," said Nadine when John reached her. "There's nobody with her right now."

"I can't thank you enough, Nadine."

"Oh, you go on and get this straightened out before it's too late," she replied as she took hold of the door handle and opened it.

John walked inside.

Clarissa stood looking out the window. She turned as she heard the door open, assuming Jane was back with her glass of water.

"What the hell?" she said as the air left her lungs.

"I can explain, Claire. Please, let me explain."

Clarissa stood momentarily staring at him, her mind seemingly frozen in time. She felt her pulse quicken, and her breathing came in short bursts.

"There's nothing to explain. Get out," she said barely above a whisper.

"Claire, I've had amnesia. I know that sounds lame. But, please, let me explain."

"Amnesia. How convenient for you."

"No really, Nadine's outside. She can explain some of it and you can even call Dr. William Mason. The night you saw me at the Café there in Northport, I got mugged when I left and apparently got hit in the head. Nadine called the ambulance. But the important thing is I remember. I remember who I am. I remember you."

Clarissa gathered up the skirt of her wedding gown and pushed passed John. She opened the door and saw Nadine.

"Nadine, honey, can you come in here, please?"

"Sure thing, Claire," Nadine replied as she slid past Clarissa. She saw John and smiled.

"Tell me what you know. And John you keep quiet."

"Well, honey, I came out of the restaurant a few nights back and found Chad laying in the alley. He'd gotten mugged. I called the ambulance and they came and got him. Took him to the hospital. I followed the ambulance to be sure he was okay."

"And?"

"And, the cops came and the doc told me he'd be okay but he was calling himself John instead of Chad and he couldn't remember a lot of stuff. Then the next thing I know they got him on the psych ward at the hospital. So I went up and visited him there and my sister, Geraldine, she's a nurse there and well, she's not supposed to tell me stuff but I forced her to tell me about Chad. Said the psychiatrist thought he was a classic case of something called fugue amnesia probably brought on by the PTSD. Said he might have some memories from being Chad but he was now back to his original self and would remember those memories instead of whoever and wherever he's been for the last fifteen years. Man, that has to be tough. To just up and lose fifteen years of your life like that."

"So he's really telling me the truth?"

"I don't know what he's told you but what I told you is the truth. Honey, I don't know what happened between you two but if you two were involved back then, you might want to listen to him before you say I do."

The door opened and Jane came scurrying back in with a glass of water.

"What's he doing here?" she asked.

"Don't ask," replied Clarissa.

"Clarissa, listen to me," said John. "I don't know how you feel about this guy you're supposed to marry but I know how I feel about you. I've loved you since the first day I set eyes on you. I remember being on my way to surprise you. Something happened. I don't know what but I knew something was missing. I never married because every time I started to ask a girl out, there was a laughing girl in my mind and it just felt wrong. I didn't understand it so I never asked anybody. I understand now. The laughing girl was you. Even when I had no clue as to who I was, I knew I loved you. I didn't know who you were or how to find you."

"But, I'm getting married." Clarissa's voiced cracked as she tried to fight back the tears.

"Claire, I asked you to marry me years ago. You said yes then. Now," John said as he bent down on one knee, "I'm asking you once again. Will you marry me?"

"John, I…"

"Sweetheart, I love you. I've always loved you ever since we were kids. Claire, honey, will you marry me?"

"Yes," she whispered as she stepped towards him.

"Hallelujah and pass the biscuits," shouted Nadine.

"Thank goodness for Christmas miracles!" exclaimed Jane as she grabbed hold of Nadine and the two hugged and danced around the room.

John stood and grabbed Clarissa around the waist lifting her off her feet and swinging her around in a bear hug. He stopped and his lips found hers.

The organist began the wedding music.

"Clarissa, honey, the music's started," said Jane. "Want me to go tell the preacher there's not going to be a wedding?"

"No, actually I need you to go get Matt. I need to talk to him."

"On my way," said Jane as she hurried out the door.

Moments later she returned with Matt in tow.

"What's going on? Are you okay, sweetheart?" said Matt as he walked through the door. "Who the hell is this?" he asked glancing at John.

"Matt, honey, I need to talk to you. Everybody else out," said Clarissa.

One by one the group exited through the doorway leaving Matt and Clarissa alone.

"Matt, honey, I'm so sorry but I can't marry you."

"What the hell do you mean?"

"I know, I know. You deserve so much better than this. That guy you saw. That's John. You remember me telling you about John."

"Yeah, he ran out on you. Left you high and dry. That guy is him? What the hell's he doing back here now?"

"Hon, I know it sounds totally absurd but he apparently had fugue amnesia. He got mugged a few nights ago and somehow hit his head, which apparently jarred his memory or something. Whatever it was, it was enough he lost the guy he was, the Chad, and regained his memory as John. That's where he's been all these years."

"So he waltzes back in here at the last minute."

"Matt, you deserve better. I know. Believe me, if I could change how I feel, I would. But it wouldn't be fair to you. I've loved John since I was two years old. I can't not marry him now."

"Damn it, Clarissa. I love you. What the hell am I gonna do now?"

Clarissa put her arms around Matt and hugged him tight.

"Somewhere, Matt, there's someone who is your soul mate. Find her."

"I love you Clarissa. I want you to be happy. You know that. But it hurts. It's going to hurt for a long time. Are you sure this is what you want?"

"Yes, Matt. This is what I want. But, for whatever it's worth, I do love you in a way. It's just that I've loved John ever since I can remember."

"I know, I know. I've seen his ghost in your eyes before. If this guy ever treats you badly …"

"You'll beat the crap out of him."

"You got that damn right," said Matt as he wiped at the moisture in his eyes. "So, I'll go tell the preacher the wedding's off."

"No, just go tell him there's been a change of grooms."

An Ethnic Christmas
by
Patrice Singleton

When the Christmas season arrives, I think of my Polish grandmother. She grew up near Krakow. Her mother died when she was sixteen, and her father married a girl her age. My grandmother left the home and got a job as a nanny for a woman in Sweden to escape life with her stepmother.

She met my grandfather who decided to go to America, and she wrote her father in Poland and told him she wouldn't be coming home. She was married and on her way to America.

Every Christmas, I make her pierogi recipe for the traditional Christmas Eve dinner and celebration held at my home. Family and friends gather to celebrate. I make pierogi only at Christmas, but my grandmother made them every Friday because she was Catholic and observed the tradition of meatless Fridays. As I begin the mixing of eggs and flour for the dough, I visualize her kitchen, bare walls and a linoleum floor.

I lived with my parents in a second-floor apartment above my grandmother's apartment. My cousin, who lived with my grandmother, and I were in charge of cleaning. Every week we scrubbed her floors and covered them with clean newspaper. In the middle of the week, we cleared the floor of newspaper. Holidays meant additional cleaning…walls were scrubbed; windows washed; every surface polished. As a grown woman with my own home and family, I find myself scrubbing and cleaning cupboards and corners, getting ready for the traditional Christmas Eve celebration with friends and family. And always celebrations centered around food.

Christmas was to be celebrated in the company of those dearest to us. Christmas tied the generations together, and the culinary traditions cemented the intimacy and love of family. In addition to pierogi, Polish ham, Polish sausage, and gingerbread, anise and lebkuchen cookies were part of an elaborate feast.

My Czech grandmother contributed the rest of the dishes for Christmas Eve. She emigrated with her husband and a young son, my father, to America just before World War I, attempting to escape extreme poverty. In America, she lost her husband to the Spanish flu, and she supported two sons by cleaning houses. Her husband (my grandfather) was twenty-six years old when he died. In her old age, she lived with my parents and me, and she fixed the traditional Czech cuisine daily. Both my parents worked, and she took care of me. It was the time of the Great Depression.

She cooked on a wood-burning stove, fixing soups and baking bread. Her recipes originated from her peasant background, and everything was made from scratch. At Christmas, she and my mother cooked and baked for days. We raised geese in our back yard, so there was goose, bread dumplings, and homemade sauerkraut and a Christmas bread, Vanoce, kolaches along with loaves of Bohemian rye bread. My annual Christmas Eve party combined the Polish and Czech cuisines.

When I was a young wife with little children, my husband and I began the Christmas Eve celebrations with family and dearest friends. For forty years, until his death, we gathered our friends and family to celebrate the season. I would begin decorating the house in November, the day after Thanksgiving. My husband and I would go to the tree farm to cut a tree. Over the years, I collected ornaments and decorations. I wanted the home to be a traditional destination for our closest friends. And as the years progressed, our friends, children and grandchildren joined the Christmas Eve party.

While my celebration was more elaborate than the traditions of my grandmother, I found the essential ingredient was the warmth and intimacy of friends and their families, as well as my own. Now, when I wander through the aisles of retail stores during the Christmas holiday season, I am astounded by the mountains of plastic decorations manufactured in China, the gaudy lights, the boxes of glass ornaments. Piles of toys, dolls, the latest tech gadgets. I am overwhelmed and feeling claustrophobic when I return home.

And I return to memories of Christmas in my childhood.

Besides the traditional foods, there were the traditional activities. I grew up poor, though I didn't know it because there was always enough food from the garden and the poultry in the back yard. My parents were frugal, and there was always love and support and not an emphasis on the material as a sign of well-being.

Ornaments were hand made. My mother would make a hole on both ends of eggs and blow out the yolks. We would paint the eggs, put a button on one end of a length of thread and pull the thread through the egg, securing the button at one end and securing the thread at the other end around a hook. A stack of colored construction paper provided the material for chains. We popped and strung popcorn. My mother popped a lot of popcorn, because we ate as much as we strung.

All year long, my mother would buy small gifts…a coloring book; crayons; pencils. She would wrap each trinket and store it in the closet. We knew the packages were there. It was part of the anticipation for Christmas. We didn't get expensive gifts, but we had lots of presents. We were ecstatic.

The best part of the Christmas season was St. Nicholas Day. The Germanic and Slavic traditions have St. Nicholas going from home to home filling stockings hung the night before. Stockings were hung on the fifth of December. My brothers and I would hang ours, and the next morning, we had a stocking full of candy, a big orange and a big apple. And a lump of coal to remind us we had not always behaved.

Like my mother, I bought gifts throughout the year for my family, practical gifts like socks, pajamas, sheets, etc. In addition to the practical items, I would buy one special gift for each person. Following the Czech tradition, we would open the gifts on Christmas Eve after everyone had left the Christmas Eve party.

In 1992, my husband was diagnosed with Parkinson's disease. My children were grown with families of their own, and I counted my blessings that I did not have to worry about supporting small children with a husband who was very ill. Eventually he had to retire from work. Over the years, I watched him slowly deteriorate physically, trembling, sometimes frozen and unable to move, and often not able to sleep.

I began to carry great sadness in my heart. There were many nights I laid awake and cried. I cried because the life we had together was gone, and I saw our destiny. I could come to terms with death and losing him, but I could not grasp what life would be without him. In the many years of our marriage and in our history together, we often knew what the other's reaction or thoughts were without ever speaking. Our life together had been a rich carpet of friends, adventure, sometimes anger, love, and children. And the future we had envisioned had vanished.

Then one year when the Christmas season arrived, I became severely depressed. I forced myself to begin decorating the house after the Thanksgiving holiday. I began the baking and menu planning, but it became a joyless task. I began to have sleepless nights, and I lost my appetite. I was at the bottom of a long dark hole without any hope. I was going to lose my husband.

One evening in that December of depression, I sat alone in the library in our home, quietly meditating on past Christmas celebrations. I wanted to sort out my sad feelings and find the strength to cope. Mentally, I returned to my childhood, to recover the feeling of security and love in my family, the traditions, the food.

As I meditated, I felt a presence in the room. My father was there, and his spirit permeated the room. His Christmas gift to me...a reminder that my childhood memories of Christmas were hope and love, not gifts and decorations and parties. His presence communicated a message. I had the inner strength to cope with my husband's illness.

The celebration of Christmas at that moment became an understanding of what role hope and love can accomplish in our journey through life.

Mystic Mistletoe
by
Malynda McCarrick

The bell over the door announced the man before she saw him enter her shop. He approached her carrying a large package, which he set on the counter with a straight face before letting his gaze scan over the items stocked on shelves behind him. She let him finish his scan, hoping against hope that he was a believer.

When he turned back to face her she found that straight face marred by a touch of disdain.

So he wasn't a believer.

Too bad.

Ivy Lovejoy's Dream Believer existed for those who wanted to be transported to the world of dreams. Her shop was filled wall-to-wall, ceiling-to-floor with shelves full of herbs and potions.

"Nice place you have here," he said with a smirk.

"Thank you," she replied with what she hoped came across as cheerful and sincere. "We like to think there is something for everyone here at the Dream Believer. Please let me know if you don't find what you are looking for and I will do my best to find it for you." That last part was delivered from her sarcastic side but with a smile. A barely audible snort escaped the man at her comments. "How may I help you?"

"I received a package that belongs to you. I just opened my shop a couple of doors down and this came when I was out." He pushed the package across the counter towards her as though its proximity to him was disgusting. It was her turn to smirk. The box was emblazoned with the sender's name, Happy Elves Mistletoe Factory.

"Oh, wonderful!" She rubbed her hands together before cracking the seal on the box. "I was getting worried that these wouldn't get here in time!" She pulled one bundle out of the box, carefully peeled the plastic wrap away from the delicate greenery and held it up in front of her. "Beautiful, don't you think?"

"Sure. You might want to double check the address they sent it to if you order from them again." And just like that he turned and stalked out of her shop. No introductions, no chance for her to thank him, and no nice-to-meet-you speech.

"Who was that?" her store clerk, Shellie Cabot, asked after the man disappeared through the front door.

"I don't know. He just brought me this. It was delivered to him by mistake." Shellie joined Ivy at the counter, flipped back the carton lid, then looked inside.

"They sent it to the wrong address. I'll get that fixed in the computer. Lucky he brought it down to you before it sat there too long."

"Yeah, we can still get them into the fridge before they get too warm and start going bad." Shellie picked up the ball of mistletoe Ivy had unwrapped and held it up for inspection.

"They always do such a nice job. These are beautiful!"

"Yes, they are going to be popular."

"So. Who do you think that guy was?"

"He says he just opened a shop a couple of doors down but he didn't bother to introduce himself or tell me anything else."

"It must be the repair shop that opened where Duffy's Candy Store used to be. That's the only thing I can think of," Shellie said. "But he didn't look like a man who liked to get his hands dirty. Maybe he's just the boss man who tells everyone else what to do and keeps his hands clean." Ivy knew how Shellie felt about men in suits. Real men got their hands dirty.

"Let's not condemn him on first impressions. He could just be having a bad day." Then she pictured his reaction to her merchandise and couldn't help smiling. "My first impression is that he is not a believer." That earned a smile from Shellie.

"We'll just have to work on changing that, won't we?"

*****

A damned voodoo shop.

Archer Boone had trusted his brother, Tag, to find him a prime location for their business, and he picked a spot two doors down from a voodoo shop! Proprietor of that shop was a red-haired, freckle-faced girl who didn't look older than fifteen.

Herbs and potions for God's sake!

The only shop that separated his from hers was a bakery.

If they hadn't already signed a lease, Archer would load everything back into his truck and move.

Too late now. The lease had been signed and marketing had already been paid for at this location. They were stuck.

"Hey, Arch. Did you meet our neighbors? What did you think?" Tag did everything with the enthusiasm of a teenager, though he had just turned twenty last year. At the ripe old age of thirty, Archer sometimes envied Tag's energy. Being the older brother had responsibilities, and having looked after his brother for most of his adult life, Archer took those responsibilities very seriously.

"I delivered the package. Didn't stick around to find out anything about them. We have work to do."

"Spoilsport. You don't know how to have fun. I tell you, I've seen the two girls running that shop and I say we need to check it out. One for me and one for you. You can have the redhead. I know you're a sucker for redheads. Perfect!"

Archer's thoughts strayed to one redhead in particular before he quickly reined them back in.

"Not all women, redhead or otherwise, are like Cynthia. Maybe it's time for you to give dating another chance," Tag said.

"Did you get all the parts unloaded and stocked?" Archer tried to get back to business, knowing how hard it was to derail his fun-loving brother when girls were the topic.

"Almost."

"Let's get that done, then. Our first client is tomorrow and we need to get organized for business."

"Alright, boss. Time to party later. I get it."

"Just keeping us on task. That phone will be ringing soon enough with new customers. We need to be ready."

"I know, I know."

"We can take a break later. How about pizza and a movie?"

"Just us or can we ask our new female neighbors?" A wink told him Tag was kidding...or at least half kidding. Yes, female companionship had been absent from Archer's life for a long time, but time spent with his brother was always good.

A low growl was all Archer could manage in response.

*****

"I have the Patterson order ready. Do you know when she planned to come by and pick it up?" Ivy didn't like to ship their merchandise to customers. Magic was fragile and didn't travel well. Shellie set the package on the counter by the cash register.

"Hopefully today before the weather gets any worse," Ivy said. They both turned to look out the shop's front display windows. "That snow is really coming down out there and I know she wanted this for her Christmas party tomorrow. She'll need the smudge sticks today, the mistletoe tomorrow."

"Do you want me to run them out to her?" Shellie loved making deliveries. It gave her the chance to get out of the shop and socialize. She was a social junkie, the perfect retail employee.

"No, we'll wait a little while and see if she makes it in."

It was a week before Christmas and business was booming. Dream Believers had a reputation for celebrating the season big, and their regular customers were never disappointed. Whether it was herbs for creating the holiday feast, sage for smudging their homes in preparation for receiving guests, or the traditional mistletoe to celebrate the season, they knew they could find it at Dream Believers.

They both turned to greet the handsome man who approached the counter with a friendly grin on his face.

"Good morning, welcome to Dream Believers. Can I help you find anything?" Shellie rushed around the counter to greet the man-boy who clearly appreciated the attention he was getting.

"Hi. I'm Taggart Boone, but you can call me Tag. Everyone does," he said and the grin now took on an impish quality. He was flirting, Shellie was enjoying it and suddenly Ivy felt older than her twenty eight years. "Me and my brother, Archer, just opened a heating and cooling repair shop two doors down. We heat things up when you're cold and cool things down when it gets too hot!"

"Nice sales pitch," Shellie flirted back with the adorable man-boy.

"Here's my card. Call anytime," Tag said with a wink and handed them each a card. "So, tell me about what you ladies do here at Dream Believers. I'm intrigued."

Shellie took him by the arm and walked him around the shop, telling him about their business. Ivy was no slouch when it came to promoting their wares, but Shellie was a genius in converting people they called non-believers, people who weren't totally on board with the idea of alternative medicine and herbal remedies.

They had been in business for five years. Shellie was hired while she was still in high school, inexperienced but enthusiastic enough that Ivy decided to take a chance on her. They grew most of their own herbs in a greenhouse at Ivy's home a short drive outside of town. What they didn't grow themselves was supplied by local growers and shipped overnight when needed.

"Shellie, I'm going to go work on the mistletoe now. Can you handle things here for a while?"

"Yeah, sure. No problem."

The mistletoe had been delivered but it wasn't ready for sale to their customers until Ivy added the special ingredient.

Magic.

*****

Archer was on his way home after a long day, during which the snow continued to fall. What he wanted was to inhale a big juicy steak and crawl under the covers of his big warm bed and sleep for a week. Starting a new furnace repair business, mid-winter, in a small town with only two men on staff was proving to be an overwhelming success, even if he was working long hours to take care of all his new customers.

Just as he turned down the road leading to that juicy steak and warm bed, his cell phone screamed for his attention. One more customer to take care of before his day was done.

He didn't recognize the name or number of the woman calling but assured her he was on his way. She was desperate. Her greenhouse had lost power and she needed it back as soon as possible or would lose all of her Christmas stock. If that didn't rate as an emergency, he didn't know what did.

He turned his truck around and headed back toward town.

Following the directions the woman had given him, the presence of a darkened greenhouse told him he was in the right place. He found it illuminated only by the full moon. The sight of a heavily bundled person running out to greet him from the front of the greenhouse had him parking his truck and getting out to meet her.

As she approached, she threw back the hood of her parka, revealing the head of unruly red hair and the freckles of the girl from the herb shop in town.

"Hi, I'm Archer Boone. Here to take a look at your heating system."

"Thank you so much for coming out so soon. This is terrible! I will lose everything if we don't get the heat back on in the greenhouse. It's supposed to drop below zero tonight! What a disaster!"

"No problem. Let's have a look at what's wrong and see what I can do to get you back up and running." His business voice. It didn't matter how he felt about the flaky girl-woman. She was now his customer so he had to play nice, treat her like any other paying customer, even though there was something about the situation that felt strangely intimate.

"We are fully stocked of Christmas goods and it is the worst time for this to happen. I keep putting off getting an emergency generator. I guess I was asking for this to happen."

Archer kept his thoughts to himself on that topic since he agreed. Trying to run a business that depended on mechanicals and not having a backup in place was asking for trouble. If he couldn't repair the system, she would find out just how badly she'd screwed up.

He got to work while she stood looking over his shoulder.

"It's not just the heating system either. The cooler seems to be acting up. It won't maintain temperatures, and I need to keep that new mistletoe shipment chilled."

He could feel her breath on the back of his neck as she chattered on. Mistletoe. Nonsense as far as he was concerned. But who was he to judge the frivolous ways people spent their money? From what he saw as he passed through the greenhouse, she had many other Christmas-related greenery in house. Why was she so specifically concerned with the mistletoe?

What did he care? He was only there to fix the heating system and get out of there as soon as possible.

There was still a juicy steak and warm bed calling to him from home.

*****

She'd called the number on the business card Tag had given her, assuming it would be Tag who would come to make the repairs. When it was his brother who stepped out of the truck, she was tempted to cancel and send him on his way, then shop around for another repairman. But the loss of everything in the greenhouse would be devastating to her business, especially during the holiday season. She was desperate. So she would play nice with Archer Boone.

She'd left the shop that afternoon to come out to the greenhouse to infuse the remaining stock of mistletoe with her special brand of magic, a love potion that worked on anyone who kissed beneath that aromatic sprig of greenery during the season of miracles. She arrived home to find the greenhouse dark and rapidly succumbing to the cold temperatures of winter outside. While the cooler temperatures were good for the mistletoe, they were deadly for the other plants growing inside the toasty walls which were normally bathed in tropical heat. Panic had her remembering the card she'd tucked in her jeans pocket earlier that day.

She leaned over Archer's shoulder as he opened the door on the power box and ran his tiny flashlight over the switches before clicking one and watching as the greenhouse was bathed in light.

"What did you find? Can you fix it?"

"I haven't looked at anything yet. I was just fixing one of your blown fuses before I look over the mechanicals." He picked up his toolbox and walked away from her without another word, leaving her to follow.

Of course she was going to follow. He wasn't offering up anything, so it was up to her to get him to talk about what he was doing. She followed at a discreet distance, far enough behind to get a good look at the man as he walked.

He stalked. There was no better way to describe how he got from one place to another. A long, confident stride that left no room for nonsense and did not encourage her to walk beside him with conversation or idle chit chat. She'd never been an idle chit chat type person anyway but the way he seemed to enjoy ignoring her was taking its toll. She'd never been pointedly ignored by somebody, nor had she ever struggled to get somebody to engage in friendly conversation. From the first moment they had met in her shop, she felt the animosity in everything he said. What had she done to deserve his attitude?

"Do you have some ideas about what could be wrong?" Another attempt to fill the awkward silence with something other than the sounds of jingling tools, work boots on paved floors, and her heartbeat pounding in her ears.

"I want to check out the heating system first."

"Then what?"

"After I see its condition I will have a better idea how to get things back up to speed."

"How long do you think that will take?"

"Are you in a hurry to be someplace?" He turned to look at her when he asked but kept walking. The heating system was located at the back of her greenhouse, housed in a smaller attached room. A utility shed. How he seemed to know where to look gave her confidence that she'd done the right thing in calling him.

"No. No hurry, just worried about my stock."

He stopped when they reached the mechanicals shed, opened the door and didn't bother hiding the disapproving click of his tongue and shake of his head as he let himself inside. This time she didn't bother following him. She'd had enough.

"I will be at the front of the greenhouse if you need me." She didn't wait for a response she knew she wouldn't get. She had a new shipment of mistletoe to check on.

*****

There was something about that woman, the woman he had initially thought to be a girl.

He snuck a look as she retreated down the cement walkway leading to the front of the greenhouse. In an innocent move of seductive bravado, she pulled off her parka and tossed it on one of the many plant tables as she passed, baring her sweater-covered, jeans-encased body for him to see. That long red hair was pulled up into a loose ponytail that teased at him as it swung from side to side, drawing his eyes down her back to her hips.

Those hips! They swayed with a natural grace with each step she took, though her steps were made choppy in her haste to get away from him.

How could he have mistaken that bombshell for a young girl? And why was he being such a jerk to a woman who had been nothing but sweet and friendly to him?

Because the alternative was impossible.

The alternative would have him sweeping the potted plants off one of her tables and laying her down, making love to her until he couldn't see straight.

*****

Her attempt at patience only served to fuel her impatience with the man. She was working on the shipment of mistletoe but her mind was on the man hidden behind the doors of her shed. Though only minutes had passed – she knew because she'd checked her watch at least ten times in the past ten minutes – it felt like hours, the tension in her shoulders and neck a painful reminder of just what was at stake here.

Not just the plants. Not just the other Christmas stock filling her greenhouse. Not just the financial investment of those goods.

Maybe it was the mistletoe.

That had to be it. She was falling under the influence of her own magic mistletoe! It made sense...except...she hadn't infused any of the mistletoe with her magic yet. Not a single one. That's what had her shaking in terror. There was something about that man.

"I have good news and I have bad news." His voice, so close...way too close...nearly made her jump out of her pants. When she was desperately trying to keep her pants on around the man, his voice was a lit stick of dynamite to her fuel-soaked brain and body. She didn't just step away from him, she jumped five feet away from him and put herself on the other side of a table just to be safe. "Which do you want first?"

Which did she want? What did she want?

Him.

He was waiting for an answer.

"Um, give me the good...I mean...the good news first."

"Okay. Your system just had a short and I was able to fix it easy enough."

"What is the bad news?"

"You really need to get a generator. I can set you up, find something that would work best for your needs and try to keep the costs down."

"Okay." That didn't sound so bad, he was offering to take care of her needs. She'd planned to get a generator for a long time but just hadn't gotten around to it, so it was no surprise. "Let's do it." Let's do it? She didn't realize she had groaned at her choice of words until she caught his reaction.

He flushed to the roots of his hair, the twitch at the corner of his mouth telling her he felt the awkwardness of the moment as much as she did.

"Um, so..." she said and absently picked up one of the mistletoe bundles she had been getting ready to work on.

"What is that?"

"This? It's mistletoe."

"Mistletoe."

"Yep. Mistletoe."

"That's the stuff people use at Christmas time to...uh..."

"Yes. Traditionally it is hung in doorways or other places in the home for luck. In modern times the tradition is to kiss somebody under the mistletoe for luck."

"For luck?"

When had he walked around the table and joined her on her side? Why hadn't she noticed that?

"Yes, for luck," she whispered, tilting her head back to hold eye contact with him as he drew near. "Luck, and other things..."

"Other things?" He dropped his voice to match hers, his eyes now holding hers captive, not allowing her to escape. "What other things?"

She watched as his face neared hers, mesmerized by the possibility of what was promised in his eyes, afraid to close hers and miss what seemed destined to happen. When everything went dark, she assumed her eyes had closed on their own.

"Damn. I'll get that fuse replaced so that won't happen again."

Spell broken.

What spell?

She hadn't even begun to cast her magic yet.

*****

"What happened last night? I tried calling for hours. I was getting worried," Shellie asked after handing Ivy the carryout tray holding their lattes. She removed hers and took her first sip.

"We lost power at the greenhouse. Had to stay up with the repairman so I didn't get home until late. Why? What did you need to talk to me about?" Ivy turned away from Shellie's probing eyes. After a lifetime of being a redhead, Ivy knew she could never hide from the truth. Her fair complexion – and tattletale blush – gave her away every time.

"You might as well tell me. I always find out the truth eventually. There was a man, wasn't there?"

"Just the repair man, nobody else."

"What repair man?"

Dang! Busted!

"Our new neighbors, the Boone brothers. Lucky we got those business cards from Tag the other day. They proved to be handy."

"So you were with Tag late last night...all alone in the dark greenhouse...trying to stay warm in a power outage?" Shellie smiled as she invented her version of the night's events. "Was that how it went down?"

"Sure. Pretty much. You guessed it."

"Liar! I was with Tag last night so that means you were with his older brother!" A giggle - laced with devilish glee - accompanied Shellie's accusation. "So? Is he a good kisser?"

"What? What do you mean? There was no kiss. What kiss? There was no kiss! No kissing!"

"Methinks thou doth protest too much."

"Shut up," Ivy muttered, then clammed up when they were joined by somebody entering the shop. Archer Boone.

"Hello, Archer! So great to see you. How are you? Can we get you anything today?" Shellie piled on the happy greeting, most likely to irritate Ivy. It did.

"Hi, Shellie. No, thanks. I just need to talk to Ivy...alone...if I could, please."

"Sure, no problem. I'll just take my coffee to the back and leave you two alone." Ivy ignored the wink and kissy face Shellie sent her before leaving them alone. The girl was due a firm scolding later. Who was she kidding? Shellie would most likely be scolding Ivy instead of the other way around.

"How can I help you?" Ivy asked in her best business voice.

"I thought I might want some of that mistletoe you were telling me about last night. Do you have any?"

What would he want with mistletoe? Did he have a girlfriend he wanted to kiss beneath the mistletoe? Of course he did! What a fool she'd been!

"Sure, I'll get you one. Wait right there."

Stiff upper lip, Ivy. It wasn't meant to be. A hunk like Archer Boone probably has a girlfriend in every town. She quickly retrieved a sprig of mistletoe and walked it to the cash register to ring it up before bundling it into one of their signature packages for him to take with him. He stopped her before they got there.

"Here, let me see that."

She handed the delicate sprig to him, watching as it nearly disappeared in his large hand, but he surprised her with the gentle way he grasped it between two fingers and raised it above his head. As she focused on the hand holding the mistletoe, she didn't see his other arm wrap around her to pull her close beneath that mistletoe.

"I'd like to hear more about the other things mistletoe is used for," he said before his mouth was on hers.

Stealing Christmas
By
Darrel Day

Two years seemed like only two days to Christall. She wasn't ready to face another Christmas without her children. Mark had insisted they put up the tree each year. He assured her it would help ease the pain and soothe her soul. He had been wrong then and he was terribly wrong this year also. The tree, with all of its lights and bulbs and popcorn strings, had only added to her heartache. She had told him how she felt and yet…

"I know it's hard for you, Christall. Do you think it's any easier for me? I miss them every single day, with all of my heart. I ask you to put the decorations out so if they should come home…"

"*If* they should come home, Mark? You can't even say the words yourself. To say "if" instead of "when" means you don't believe strongly enough to say "when." I will never get on with life until the day we find them. And no, by God…they are not gone forever. Every day I search for clues as to who took them and where they are now. To give up is to say we didn't care enough to keep searching."

Mark looked at his wife and felt his heart sink. She was only a shadow of the woman he had held two years ago. She ate only enough to stay alive, and he wasn't sure she even ate enough for that. He wondered sometimes if perhaps she really didn't care if she lived or died. He reached for her, sorry for the hurtful words he again had spoken.

Holding her tight, Mark whispered in her ear, "I love you, Christall, and we will never stop searching for our children. Not ever."

Pushing Mark away, Christall walked to the large picture window in their living room. She stared out at the falling snow, watching as it blanketed the ground and trees. She wrapped her arms around herself and shivered. Feeling tears flow down her cheeks, she wiped them away, angry she couldn't stop them. She truly believed the kids were still out there. The police, her friends and family had told her she needed to move on. She tried but it simply didn't happen. Inside of her heart, Christall still needed to believe, because to stop would end her reason for living.

Christall heard a knock on the door. She looked out the living room window to see who it was. The snow was coming down harder and the wind suddenly picked up. Who would be out in the middle of nowhere in these conditions? She heard the door open and close without hearing anyone speak.

"Who was at the door?" She waited for a response but there was none. "Mark?" she called out as she walked towards the front door. She found Mark staring down at something in his hand.

"Are you deaf or just ignoring me again? I asked you who was…"

Christall looked down as Mark held his hand out to show her a small piece of cloth. She reached out slowly and took it. She felt dizzy and thought she might pass out. She held the material to her face, rubbing it against her cheek softly. This time she didn't try to stop the tears.

"Where did this come from?"

"The mailman brought it to the door."

Christall opened the door and looked outside. The mail truck was just leaving.

"The wind is covering his tracks quickly. Didn't think mail would be running in this weather. This is the scarf Mary was wearing the day she and Logan disappeared. Remember she insisted we find it for her the night before. She still had it on at the store. I remember telling her not to leave it lying on one of the counters."

"But did she have it on when you saw her last?!"

"Don't raise your voice, Mark. I'm not a child. Yes. She was wearing it around her waist like a belt."

"It doesn't make sense at all. We're going to call the police right now. Maybe they can get fingerprints or some whatever it is, DNA, off of the scarf or the envelope."

For the first time since the kids had disappeared, Christall hugged Mark tight. She held him as if she were afraid he might pull away. She was glad he squeezed back.

"Mark…I'm so sorry for all I have put you through. I have been so afraid of every knock on our door."

"I know, my love, but maybe now we can face this together."

*****

Two years earlier

"All right kids, we need to get ready to go. I told your Aunt Carla we'd meet her in thirty minutes. She'll be upset if we're late again. She has very little patience and I don't want to start out with a fight."

Logan and Mary put their coats on. Logan stopped to look at the Christmas tree. He loved when it was lit up at night. He would shut off all the lights except for the tree lights. Sitting in front of the tree, the fireplace warming the room, he would try to guess what was in the boxes. Of course not all of the gifts were under the tree yet. Santa wouldn't bring their gifts until Christmas Eve.

Mary had tried to tell him Santa wasn't real. She said she knew because she was older than Logan by four years. At twelve years old, his sister thought she knew everything. But Logan knew she was wrong about Santa.

In the car, Mary began poking fun at Logan again. He wished his mother would tell her to just shut up.

"Mother, please tell baby Logan that you and Dad are Santa. I'm tired of hearing him try to guess what Santa might bring him."

Logan waited to hear what his mother would say. He believed everything she told him; after all, she was his mother.

"Will you stop teasing your brother? You know as well as I do, Santa is real. Leave him alone before you really upset him."

"Really, Mother. Are you going to lie to this poor little boy? He's old enough to know the truth."

"She already answered you, Miss Know-It-All." Logan did what every boy his age would do. He stuck his tongue out at his sister as she crossed her arms in front of her in a huff.

At the store, Logan stayed close to his mother's side. He didn't like stores or trust people. Mary walked behind Logan as Christall and their aunt talked about anything and everything.

Logan looked back once and didn't see Mary. He stopped to see if she were hiding in the clothes racks. She liked to do that and then jump out and scare him. He was determined he would not be scared this time. Moving clothes from side to side, he waited for her to pounce out at him like a tiger. But rack after rack, Logan found no one hiding inside the clothes. He heard a woman's voice from behind one of the racks.

"I think your sister is sick. I saw her running to that bathroom holding her hand over her mouth."

Logan looked at the woman and then at the bathroom marked Family. He could see his mom and aunt walking and talking. He called out to them.

"I'm just going to check on Mary, Mom. She went into the bathroom. It will only take a minute." Logan saw his mother turn around and look at him.

"We'll stand here and wait for you both. Please tell her to hurry. We have other places to go."

Logan nodded and rushed towards the bathroom. The woman who had told him about Mary was nowhere to be seen. He knocked on the door.

"Mary, are you in there? Mom said for you to hurry so we can go." Logan waited for an answer and then pulled the door open. As he looked inside, he saw the lady who had told him about Mary.

"Where's my sister? You said she came in here." Logan felt something wet on his face. It took his breath away and he suddenly became dizzy. He felt himself being pulled into the bathroom as his world went dark.

*****

As Christall and Mark waited for the detective, she thought back to that horrible day.

How did the woman get Logan and Mary out of the store? Most of what the police know is assumptions. Even the customers and store employees who swore they saw the whole thing gave different descriptions of the woman with the kids. People described two women helping two kids outside. They told onlookers their children were diabetic and having a low sugar episode. One of the women even asked if someone could get a manager to help them. The women were gone by the time the lady returned with a manager.

How could so many people see so many different things? Ten different descriptions of the escape vehicle left very little for the police to go on. No one even got a plate number.

The news had said: Three days before Christmas, two young children named Logan and Mary Pierce disappeared without a trace. Pictures of Logan and Mary were shown on every channel and put up across town.

Christall blamed herself for not following Logan to the bathroom, but twenty-five feet didn't seem like too far away to let him get his sister. Everything happened in a matter of five minutes. By the time Christall reached the bathroom it was empty.

*****

Soon Christall and Mark were sitting at their kitchen table with the detective assigned to the case.

"We're going to need to keep the scarf and envelope. I'll have the lab test the envelope for prints. It's been two years since the children went missing but it's still listed as an open case because it involves kids. I just don't want you to hang your hopes on finding anything."

"We understand, sir. Can you tell us if there was ever a lead that simply didn't come through for you?"

"We spoke with a couple who had given us a lead shortly after the disappearance. They claimed to have seen your daughter in a van a few counties over. We did a full search but found nothing that matched their description. No one ever said they saw a van associated with the store abduction before. We continue to follow any lead we get no matter how insignificant it may seem."

"That's reassuring, sir."

"Please call me Leon, ma'am. I promise to get back to you if I find anything. There was something else we looked into but it didn't pan out. The day the kids were taken, you said there was a car tailgating you in the parking lot."

"Yes, it was a man and woman that we assumed were trying to get to a parking spot before us. They were in a pickup truck, not a car. We passed one spot so they would leave us alone but they drove past it, too. We took another spot and saw them park one row over from us. My sister Carla gave you a description of the truck and the plate number."

"We followed up on that but the plates didn't exist in any motor vehicle files. We are sure it was a fabricated plate. Had you ever seen the truck before?"

"I didn't think I had but a few days later I saw one that looked the same at another store. I ran up to it but there was an older couple driving it. I assumed I had made a mistake."

"I'm going to do more checking on that and will let you know," the detective said, as they all stood.

Mark and Christall shook the detective's hand. Then the door closed and he was gone.

Sleep barely came to either of them that night. Every sound caused them to sit straight up in bed. They could hear the wind howling outside the house.

Mark was out of bed before daylight. The snow had drifted across their drive, high enough to close off where the end met the highway. Mark thought he saw something move near the mailbox. He sipped his coffee and watched closely. He saw the mail truck pulling away and called out to Christall.

"I am going to the mailbox, but I need you to watch for me. The snow is drifted and if I fall I might need some help."

"What the hell are you doing?"

"Just watch for me, okay? I'll be back in a minute or two."

Christall watched as Mark drudged through the three foot drifts. Her heart raced when she saw him fall into a drift. She jerked the door open just as he stood. He made it to the end of the drive, removed something from the mailbox and tore it open.

When he got back to the house, Mark was covered in snow except for the arm he had tucked into his coat. Christall felt her legs nearly go out from under her when he pulled his arm out and showed her the jacket Logan had been wearing when he was taken. She grabbed it from him and hugged it to her face. Logan's scent was still on it.

Mark showed her a note that had been pinned to it. She read the note and then slid down to the floor.

"What the hell is going on here? Did you read this?"

Mark nodded. "I did, and I think we should do exactly what the note says."

"Do you believe we could actually find them, after all this time?"

"I never believed anything else. We can't afford to waste any time.

We'll leave a note next to the one we just got. Your sister will call and when she doesn't hear back from you, she'll come here."

"But the note says not to…"

"I know what the note says, but we need to be sure we have the kids by then. We have to let someone know where we are in case things don't go as planned."

*****

After bundling up, they put blankets and food in the Silverado. Christall wrote a note to her sister and they left. They were both nervous but neither said so to the other.

Mark drove down the snow-covered highway towards a side-road he knew from hunting. It would take them deeper into the forest.

"Do you remember the cabin the note mentioned, Mark? How could they be so close and us not know?"

"It doesn't matter now. It only matters that we find them and bring them home."

The road began to narrow as Mark struggled to keep the vehicle on it. The trees closed in around them like a blanket as the light slowly faded. The forest went on for miles, each turn getting tighter. Suddenly the back of the truck began to slide sideways. Mark tried to keep it on the road, a battle he knew he had already lost.

"Hold on tight, Christall!"

In that instant, Mark felt the vehicle connect with the trees. There was a loud scraping sound as branches chewed through Christall's door and cracked against the windshield.

Christall screamed as the windshield shattered, covering her in glass. As suddenly as it started, the sliding was finished and the Silverado rested against a tree. Mark looked over at Christall. Blood trickled down her face.

"Oh God, baby, your forehead is cut! I need to put something on that."

Christall pressed her fingers against the cut. "I'll be fine but I need to get out on your side."

"Luckily we aren't far from the cabin. It'll be dark soon so let's grab a bag and put a few things in it. We can take some food and blankets with us."

Christall watched as Mark slid his hunting rifle out from behind the seat.

"We need to take this with us. There are wolves in this area and I don't want to take a chance."

Christall knew why Mark really wanted the rifle. She felt the same way. They slowly began walking towards the cabin. Mark carried a flashlight with him, knowing darkness wasn't far away. The wind had picked up, impeding their trek even more.

"What if we get there and they're…" The words caught in her throat, "…not in the cabin?"

"We're not leaving this forest without our kids. We'll search until we find them."

Darkness came sooner than they wanted. Mark followed the beam of the flashlight. His keen sense of smell told him wolves were nearby. He'd caught their scent shortly after exiting the Silverado but didn't mention it to Christall.

"It feels like something's watching us. Please tell me we'll be at the cabin soon," Christall said as she shivered from the cold.

Mark knew the wolves would be nearby. It had been an extremely cold winter making their food source nearly non-existent. Wolves had attacked a neighbor's livestock less than a week ago. A hungry wolf didn't care what filled its stomach.

Mark heard a low growl somewhere in the forest. The volume told him the wolf was close. He aimed the rifle towards the sound.

"Just keep walking. We are being followed. Here, you carry the flashlight and walk in front of me. The cabin should be just past the next stand of trees."

Just then, Christall tripped over a branch bent to the ground by the heavy snow. The flashlight crashed into a tree trunk. She felt her heart skip as the light went out. Mark stepped ahead and picked it up, shaking it while turning it off and on.

"Shit! That takes care of the flashlight. I guess we walk in the dark."

"I'm sorry. I didn't mean to drop it."

"It is alright, baby. Just keep moving."

They walked until the cabin came into view. There was a van parked outside. The wolves had moved closer to the edge of the trees. Mark aimed the rifle in the direction of their movement. He knew if they were very hungry, the wolves would not be afraid to attack.

"The note said the kids would be waiting for us inside. Why are we standing here, Mark?"

"I want to make sure it's safe to go in."

Mark moved into a clearing in front of the cabin, his rifle ready for use. A large wolf stepped out of the trees. Mark took aim just as two more wolves stepped into the clearing.

"Walk slowly to the door, Christall."

Christall did as she was told without hesitation. Mark moved towards her, watching the wolves as he did. Suddenly, the first wolf lunged. Firing a round as quickly as he could, Mark watched the wolf collapse at his feet.

He felt the bite before he saw it happen. A second wolf had managed to slip in and latch on to Mark's forearm. Using the butt of the rifle, Mark smashed it into the wolf's head. With a yelp, the wolf released Mark's arm. Blood oozed from the bite as Mark aimed and fired again. The wolf fell silent to the ground. The third wolf retreated to the safety of the trees.

"Mark, you're hurt badly!"

"No, he didn't get a good grip on my arm. I'll live. If anyone is inside, though, they know we're here now. We need to get in there. When I nod, open the door."

They looked into each other's eyes and then Mark nodded. Christall opened the door and stood back. Mark entered the cabin, pointing his rifle around the room. Christall followed Mark in and shut the door behind her.

A blazing fireplace warmed the room. There were two closed doors and a wall blocking their view, leaving them no way to know if there was anyone inside.

Mark heard footsteps as a woman stepped out into view. He pressed his finger against the trigger. The woman appeared to be about Mark and Christall's age. She looked frail and weak as she leaned on the wall. She was in a dress that looked like a throwback to the seventies. Her long blonde hair was neatly brushed. Her voiced trembled as she spoke.

"There won't be any need for that rifle. I couldn't fight you if I wanted to."

Mark kept the rifle aimed her way. Christall rushed forward and shoved the woman against the wall, holding her up by her arms. The woman stared into Christall's anger-filled eyes.

"Where are my kids, you piece of shit? I want to know what you did with my babies!"

"They're safe and warm. I'll show them to you as soon as I explain why I told you where we were."

"I don't care why you called us here. I just want my kids back. Now!"

Christall let go of the woman's arms, watching her fall to the floor. She pushed open the first door, half expecting to see her kids. Instead, she saw a man lying on a bed. Christall knew immediately he was dead. Glazed eyes stared up at the ceiling, dried blood covering his face and bare chest. The shirt he wore looked as if it had been through a shredder.

"What the hell happened to him?" Christall asked.

"That's my husband. He was attacked a week ago by the same wolves you just fought off. They nearly killed him before he reached the cabin. I took ill from going out in the cold trying to get food for the kids. I was afraid I might die so I sent you the clothes and the note."

"Why didn't you just let the kids go?" Mark asked.

His voice was filled with anger as he moved to the second door. Pushing it open, his heart sank when he found the room empty.

"You said the kids would be here when we got here! Where the hell did you put them?"

He pointed the rifle down at the woman. It was near enough for her to see straight into the barrel. He held it there, waiting for her response.

She coughed and wheezed, barely able to breathe.

"I didn't want to give them back to you. When Leo died, it left me no choice. The kids were told if one escaped, we would take the other one far away from here. Neither of them ever dared try to run away. They never knew how close to their home they were. We lost our son and daughter in an accident three years ago. My husband knew I was lonely for my children. We would drive by your home and see them waiting for their school bus. Leo decided we should take them and raise them as our own. I would have never contacted you if he hadn't died. Luck was with me that the mail was still running. The scarf, the jacket and the note were my only way of letting you know where we were."

"You still haven't told us where they are! I don't want to talk any more. Tell us or I swear I will shoot you right here."

"Do that and you won't ever find them."

"Just tell us, please. My husband and I want our kids back."

Mark could see a shed near the cabin. "Did you put them out in the shed, you bitch? Damn you to hell!"

"They are nearby. You will find them quite safe and healthy. All you have to do is get past the wolf pack you pissed off. I hope you do make it to them safely. All I wanted was to love them and call them my own."

"They were never yours to call anything. You kidnapped our children and kept them from us for two years! We've spent two Christmases without them. I hate you for that and I don't care if you live or die!"

The woman looked at Christall and nodded at her words.

"I was sure you were going to say that so I prepared a backup plan for me so I would not have to face jail. Take my van when you leave. The keys are inside. I do hope you can get back home safely."

She stood up and stepped into the room her husband was in. She pushed her hand inside her pocket, pulled out a revolver, and in a single move put the revolver under her chin and pulled the trigger. Christall screamed as blood splattered onto the walls. The woman dropped to the floor, her dead eyes staring up at them, very little else of her face recognizable anymore. Mark dragged her body further into the room, far enough to close the door. He didn't want the kids to see her. He reached out to Christall and held her body close to his own.

"We need to know if the kids are in that shed." Sounds of scratching outside told them the wolves were still very much there. "You stay inside and I will shoot my way to the shed."

"No, no, Mark, I'm going with you."

"You must be ready to let us inside when I get the kids out. If something happens to me, I need you to wait out the wolves until help comes. If I know your sister, help is already on the way."

Christall nodded and then kissed Mark.

"Go get them, Mark, so we can go home."

Mark opened the door a little and looked outside. The wolves were trying to dig their way into the cabin, but they were not near the door now. Mark could see the shed from where he stood. He knew he had only one chance to reach it.

Suddenly, they both heard a sound coming from somewhere down the hallway. Closing the door, Mark walked down the hall. A second room was just past the bathroom. Mark opened the door slowly. As he did, he found himself staring into the eyes of his children. Bound and gagged, they seemed in a daze at seeing their father. Logan waited for his father to untie him. He hugged him as Mark freed Mary.

"Dad, the woman is going to find you here and kill you! She told us she would do it!"

"You don't need to worry about her anymore, Logan."

Hearing Logan's voice, Christall burst through the door and grabbed both of her children. She kissed them and held them tight.

"We've found you! What a perfect Christmas gift this is."

"It's time to go now. I don't want you kids in this cabin all night. We need to reach that van before the wolves reach us. When I say run, you run as fast as you can."

Mark opened the door and seeing no wolves, he told Christall and the kids to run for the van. The wolves appeared from behind the cabin and began to chase them. Mark fired three rounds off, killing one of the big males. His second shot missed its intended target. Christall heard the gunfire as she opened the van's door. She grabbed the kids, pulling them inside just as Mark jumped in and closed his door.

One large wolf struck Mark's door hard. It stared in the window at Mark, licking its snout as it did. Christall held her children tight and cried. Mark wrapped his arms around them all, holding them close.

"How are we going to get past the wolves, Dad?

"We are going to drive right past them, Logan. I have faith your Aunt has sent someone to get us."

Mark drove until he saw headlights shining through the trees. He could hear the echo of snowmobiles coming towards them. Moments later, he stood face to face with Leon, whose smile was as warm as a fireplace.

"You took a hell of a chance," Leon said. "Christall's sister told us where to find you."

"It was about finding our children, Leon. Would you have done anything less? There are two bodies in the cabin up ahead. One died from an attack by wolves; the other was self-inflicted."

"My men will go up there and take care of it all. Let's bundle you up and get you all back home. My boys will figure a way to get your vehicle back to you. You can tell me what all happened later."

"Thank you for coming to find us, sir."

Leon smiled at Logan.

"It's what we do, son. I'm just glad to see all of you."

*****

The next three days passed quickly. Logan came running into his mom and dad's bedroom before sunrise. He tugged at them both, trying to pull them from their bed.

"Get up so we can see what Santa left for me!"

Mark rolled over, smiling at Logan.

"What's the hurry, buddy?"

"Don't you want to see what Santa left for us?"

Mary walked into the bedroom yawning and stretching.

"You might as well get up, Dad. He isn't going to stop until he opens his gifts."

Christall turned to face the kids. She snuggled up to Mark and kissed him.

"Aw, no more smooching, guys. There are gifts out there."

Mark pulled both kids over on top of him and Christall.

"Those gifts will wait for a minute or two. Right now, your mom and me are holding the only gifts we will ever need on Christmas day."

"Your dad is right. You two are the best Christmas gifts we could ask for."

Eight Days Before Christmas
By
Birdie Hawks

Hearing her doorbell ring, she walked to the door and opened it. There stood Jake, all man. She knew him as the retired veterinarian who helped his dad around her property. She took a deep breath and held it. Her nipples hardened and rubbed against her t-shirt.

"How many times have I thought about him making love to me?" she thought.

He opened the outside door.

"I just wanted to make sure you were ok."

She took a step back.

He took a step in and looked down at her.

She leaned against his hardened chest and he...

Trudy Kerns awoke with a start as her two dogs started barking crazily. She blew out the breath she had been holding for what seemed like hours.

"What the heck is your problem?" Breathing heavily she looked over at her dogs. They were moving around erratically, causing a startled Trudy to sit up in bed. "This is a strange time for you guys to go out!" She glanced over at the clock on her night stand. Midnight! *You're kidding me!*

"Shut up, you two! I'm coming." She threw back the covers and slid her legs off the bed as her dogs ran from the bedroom, barking all the way. After stepping into her slippers, she followed them into the kitchen.

She turned on the light over the kitchen table and tipped her head as muffled sounds of sirens came to her. *That's a strange sound to hear in the country. I wonder what's going on?*

Her dogs were dancing around the front door. They never went out front, so the sirens must be getting close. Since her front porch was enclosed, she walked through the living room and opened the door. They ran out and she followed. The scene she saw took her breath away.

Fire trucks, several sheriffs' cars and an ambulance were pulling in across the road while orange flames leaped from the old white farm house, blasting into the black night sky. A stunned Trudy rushed back into her house, called her dogs in and hurried to her bedroom.

*****

Having put on warm clothes, coat, boots, gloves and hat, Trudy went out her front door and headed down her lane to the gravel road in front of her house. As she approached a deputy standing in the road he held up his hand for her to stop.

"You can't get any closer, ma'am."

"I'm Trudy Kerns. Is the lady who lives there, Joy Gibson, okay?"

"I think so, Ms. Kerns. She said her little dog got her attention and they got out."

Trudy let out a deep breath of relief. "Where is she?"

"She's at the ambulance being checked out. Do you know if anyone else was there?" he asked.

"Her girls are both away at college. They aren't expected home for a couple more days yet." Trudy glanced at his name sewn on his jacket. "Can I get her, Deputy Howard? She can stay with me."

"Only if the EMT says she's okay."

Trudy and the deputy walked to the ambulance. Joy sat inside the rescue unit, shaking, a blanket wrapped tightly around her.

"Joy!" Trudy exclaimed. The head of Joy's little dog peaked over the top of the blanket.

"Trudy," Joy rasped out, as tears flowed down her cheeks.

"Can Mrs. Gibson come home with me?" Trudy asked, the EMT. "We're friends and I live right across the road."

"I see no reason why not. Her lungs are clear. But, if she starts having breathing problems, call 911 and we'll come back," the EMT explained.

"I'll walk you ladies home when she's done signing a release form," the deputy said. Once Joy had finished the paperwork, he stepped up to the unit and helped her down.

"Thanks, Officer," Trudy said.

"Yes. Thank you, Officer," Joy said.

When they got to the front door, Trudy turned to the officer. "Would you like to come in for a cup of coffee?"

"Thanks, but I can't. Still on duty."

"Of course. Well, thanks for the help, sir."

The officer nodded, turned and walked away.

For a few moments, Trudy watched him leave and thought of her husband, a thirty-year police veteran. Tears welled up in her eyes and she blinked rapidly to clear them.

"Come on, Joy. Let's get in."

Trudy took Joy's small dachshund from her arms and set her on the tiled floor where she promptly peed. "I'll get that later. Let's get you inside the house, Joy."

Joy stood motionless, clutching the blanket. Trudy moved to face her friend, hands grasping Joy's upper arms.

"Joy!" she said, softly, "Snap out of it. Are you okay?"

Joy blinked her eyes several times and took a deep breath, letting it out in a whoosh. "I'm okay. I just feel so bad about the house."

"Don't worry about that." Trudy guided her friend into the house.

Joy's dog ran ahead and was greeted by Trudy's dogs, their barks mixing wildly as they ran down the hall ahead of the women.

"Let's have some hot chocolate," Trudy said, as she took her cold weather clothes off at the hall closet.

"Sounds good to me," Joy said, still clutching the blanket. "How am I going to return this blanket to the ambulance people?"

Wrapping her arm around Joy's shoulders, Trudy walked her down the hall to the kitchen.

"They have expendable things. Some officers even have blankets and teddy bears in their trunks," Trudy stated. "Take a seat at the table." In the butler's pantry, Trudy got two hot chocolate pods out of a drawer, poured water into the coffee maker, and slid a cup under the spout.

Joy sat at the kitchen table. The blanket slid off her shoulders as she laughed at the three dogs running out of the family room, through the kitchen, down the hall, into the laundry room, back up the hall, through the kitchen and back into the family room.

Trudy stood still with cups of hot chocolate in the air waiting for the dogs to get by. She set a cup down in front of Joy and then sat in her chair.

"You must be warming up," she said as Joy sipped the hot liquid.

"I feel a lot better."

"Good! Did you call the girls yet?" Trudy asked.

"Yes. I used the EMT's phone. Mine's in the house. They wanted to come right home, but I told them to wait because of the weather."

"Good idea. They can stay here too."

"We really couldn't put you out, Trudy."

"I insist," Trudy said.

*****

The next morning, Trudy sat at the kitchen table watching the weather on the news. "Looks like it's going to get worse before it gets better."

"Wow!" Joy exclaimed, as she set a scrambled egg down in front of Trudy.

"Thanks. Looks good," Trudy told Joy.

The house phone rang. Trudy got up and answered it.

"Hello, Officer Howard. What's happening? Oh, my gosh! Are they okay? Are you sure they can make it here? Okay. I'll open my garage door." She hung up.

Eyebrows knitted, Joy stood looking at Trudy. "What happened?"

"Deputy Howard said a school bus with kids slid off the road and so did he when he went to help them. They are walking here. I'm going to the garage to meet them. Will you make up some soup and hot drinks?"

"Sure, Trudy."

*****

Trudy pushed the button for each of the three garage doors and pulled her truck and both cars to the garage door opening. In each vehicle she turned on the flashing hazard lights and put the headlights on high.

Even with her coat and boots on, she shivered and squinted into the white wall of snow, hoping to get a glimpse of them. Is that them?

"Yes!" she hollered. Her phone rang. "I think I see you. Yes, those are my cars." She hung up and called Joy. "I see them."

It seemed to take forever for them to get there, but they finally did. "Hi, Officer. Everyone please come in!"

The young people filed by her. Most weren't dressed properly for Iowa in the winter. One had a short skirt, no coat, no shoes. Trudy shook her head. A shaking woman whom Trudy guessed to be in her forties walked up to her.

"Thank you! I'm Martha, the bus driver."

Trudy reached out and rubbed her upper arms. "You're welcome, Martha." Trudy looked around. "Is everyone accounted for?"

Martha said, "I counted eight. That's all of them and some need medical treatment."

"We'll do what we can," Trudy said, looking at the officer. "Will you please turn off my cars and truck and shut the garage doors?"

"Sure."

"This way, everyone." Trudy gestured toward the door leading to the breezeway. "Excuse me," she said, as she walked through the crowd. "Follow me, kids." Trudy noticed the girl who was barely dressed. Her teeth were chattering and she was bent over and pale. Another girl had her arms around her. Trudy put her hand on the girls back. "Come on in. We'll get you warmed up."

Everyone filtered into the warm breezeway. Trudy stopped at the closed door going into the house. "Everyone get your coats, hats, gloves and footwear off. Please hang your coats in the closet or on the coat trees."

"What are coat trees," one of the boys asked.

"These are coat trees." Trudy patted one of the poles that stood in the breezeway, hung her coat from a hook, and slipped off her boots.

Martha hung her coat next to Trudy's, slipped off her boots and gloves and left them on the floor.

"But I'm too cold to take my coat off," a girl said.

Trudy looked at her. "My house is warm. You'll be just fine except for the icicle here." She patted the overly cold girl on the back. "But we'll fix her too."

The kids did as they were told. The officer walked into the breezeway but only took off his boots, hat and gloves.

"I have a room you can put your coat and utility belt in," Trudy told him in a low voice.

· He nodded. "Thanks," he said, his voice equally quiet. "I didn't want to leave it unattended."

"Down the hallway is the kitchen. There are hot drinks and soup waiting for you," Trudy told the kids and watched them as they headed down the hall.

"Officer, you can put your gear in my office and lock the door. It's just inside the door on the left. I'll bring you the key."

"Please call me Nelson."

"Almost everyone has their injuries tended to," Nelson told Trudy as he walked into the kitchen.

"Let me guess. The icicle," Trudy said.

Going into the family room, Martha and Trudy walked over to the sitting on the sofa with a blanket wrapped around her.

"This is Sue," Martha introduced as she sat on the girl's right. "And this is her best friend, Deb."

Trudy sat on the coffee table in front of Sue. The girl's face was still pale.

"Have you had anything to eat or drink, Sue?" Martha softly asked.

The girl said nothing, but Deb said, "She hasn't had anything. I think she's very sick."

Trudy leaned toward the girl. "You need to get up and walk."

Sue slowly shook her head.

"If you're going to get better…You do want to feel better don't you?" Trudy asked.

Sue nodded.

"We have no access to medical services, so it's up to us." Trudy stood and offered her hands to the girl, who briefly hesitated and then took them. "Now, stand up."

On unsteady legs, Sue rose. Deb, Martha and Trudy made sure she didn't fall.

"Now take a step," Trudy said. "Look at me."

Sue made eye contact with Trudy.

"Let's first go over to that table and get you some hot chocolate," Trudy said, as she guided Sue. "Walking will get your circulation going in your legs and feet. And hey, chocolate is good for everything. Right?"

Sue smiled.

Luckily, the walk wasn't far and Joy set a cup of creamy hot chocolate on the small table near the fireplace as Sue sat.

"Just sip it slowly," Trudy said.

The other kids struck up conversations with Sue and even made her laugh a little.

Trudy left the family room and walked into the kitchen where Nelson and Martha were drinking soup. Joy handed her a cup of mocha coffee before she sat.

"Thanks, Joy." She took a sip, relishing the warmth and chocolate. "So, Nelson. Any word on the weather?"

"Right now everything is at a standstill. Snow's not expected to stop until sometime this evening," he said.

"So tell me about the accident, Nelson. What happened when you got to the bus?"

"I checked the kids out and decided they couldn't stay in the bus because it was tilted too badly. I remembered you were close so I got everyone out and here we are. Everything is so disorienting in a blizzard. There's no sense of direction."

"I know. I walked in one when I was a stupid teenager. Luckily my brother was close by and brought me home. That's why I opened my garage doors and turned on my car lights. I knew what you were going through."

"That sure helped," he said.

"So what do we do about sleeping tonight?" Martha asked.

Just then, one of the boys came in. "I think you better check Sue out."

Everyone at the table jumped up and headed into the family room. Sue was moaning loudly and crying.

Trudy looked at Sue's face and felt it. "Are your feet hurting really bad?"

"Yes! Please make it stop."

Nelson said, "Your feet may be frost bit. Unfortunately, when they thaw out it hurts like the devil."

Trudy looked up at Nelson. "Bath?"

"Warm one. Not hot," he said.

"Let's get you up, Sue," Trudy said. She looked at Sue's friend. "Come with us."

*****

Trudy opened the door to the master suite and three over-excited dogs jumped and barked at them.

"Dogs!" Sue's friend screeched.

"Yeah! Yeah! Warm up first. Dogs second," Trudy said. "Joy. Will you make the dogs go out back in the screened in porch, please?"

Joy picked her dog up and called the other two. They followed her down the hall to the breezeway. Trudy herded Martha and the girls into the master bath.

"Let me get some water in the tub," Trudy said. "You're going to have to take your clothes off, Sue."

"I thought I'd just soak my feet."

"Have to raise your core temp. Deb can stay in here with you. We'll be just outside the door if you need help." Trudy turned off the water. "Do not add hot water. I'll get you sweatpants, sweatshirt and socks."

Closing the door behind her, Trudy and Martha stood just outside. "I'll get that stuff and be right back," Trudy said.

*****

A while later, Sue and Deb came out of the bathroom. Sue had color back in her face and she was walking on her own.

"Feeling better?" Martha asked.

"Yes. At first, I was skeptical about the water, but it really helped. I'm hungry."

That's a good sign. Trudy put her hand on top of Sue's shoulder. "Winter. Iowa."

"Yes. I know. I'll dress better from now on. The pain of thawing out was terrible."

"Lesson learned," Trudy said.

"Now, where are the dogs?" Sue asked.

"In the family room begging, of course," Trudy said.

Trudy and Martha walked back to the kitchen as the girls rushed to the family room.

The kids had the big screen TV over the fireplace blasting. Trudy walked in there and picked up the remote from the coffee table. She hit the mute. The kids moaned. Trudy looked around the room before addressing them.

"We have to share the same spaces for at least 24 to 48 hours before we can get dug out."

Another moan from the kids.

"The TVs will have low volume."

One boy said, "TVs? Plural?"

Another one said, "As more than one?"

"Yes. But more important, Martha has brought up a question about the sleeping arrangements tonight. Oh, and I hope you all have contacted your folks to let them know you're ok."

They all acknowledged that they had.

"Now, as I started to say, Martha and the girls will sleep upstairs. Joy will take you up to check it out. Nelson and the boys will stay in the basement. I will take you down there and show you around. Let's go." Trudy turned and headed out of the family room.

From just inside the family room doorway, Joy said, "This way, girls."

*****

Trudy headed down the steps with Nelson, and the boys followed.

As the guys entered the basement, there were sounds of joy as they looked at the big screen TV, pool table, juke box and poker table.

"I have my grandkids over and we come down here and play," Trudy said. "Here are the rules."

The four boys got quiet.

"Keep the sound down and ten is bedtime."

"Why so early?" one of the boys asked.

"Because tomorrow we may be digging ourselves out and you'll need your rest. Eating and drinking will be done at the table. There may be more rules as we go along but you're seventeen and shouldn't need to be told common sense things. But, you may have to be reminded off and on. Anyway, the sofa folds out, we have sleeping bags if you sleep on the floor and you can sleep in the recliners."

*****

Martha and two of the girls were just coming down from the upstairs when Trudy came up from the basement.

"Well, is that going to work?" Trudy asked Martha.

"It will be great," one of the girls said.

One of the girls was carrying Trudy's small dog, Squirt. "Can I have her?"

"I'm afraid not," Trudy said, as she took her dog. Turning, she walked to her bedroom and closed the door.

Sue watched her go. "Trudy seems sad," she stated.

"Well, tomorrow is her birthday."

"What's with the naked Christmas tree in her living room?" Deb questioned.

"It's been up since the first." Joy walked to the kitchen and started rinsing the dishes and putting them in the dishwasher.

Sue and Deb followed her. "Can we help?" they asked.

"I never turn down help."

"I don't think I'd like to have a birthday eight days before Christmas," Sue said.

"Me neither," Deb said. "Probably don't get as many presents so close to Christmas."

Joy stopped working and said, "She lost her husband a year ago. And wasn't even going to decorate for the holidays. She got a tree but that's as far as she got."

*****

The boys were still in the basement so the girls cleaned up the family room and kitchen. Trudy came out of her room and joined them.

When they were finished, Trudy said, "Why don't you kids go downstairs and have some fun. Lights out at 10."

Sue's phone rang and she walked away from everyone to talk.

*****

Trudy, Joy and Martha were sitting at the kitchen table talking and watching the weather on the TV when Deb rushed up to them.

"Come quick. I think Sue's sick again!" she gasped. "She's in the laundry room."

The ladies jumped to their feet and headed down the hall. Upon entering, Trudy crouched down to Sue who was sitting on the floor crying.

"What's wrong, icicle?"

"My...sister," Sue choked out. "She's lost in the storm."

"Where?" Martha asked.

Sue gasped for air. "She's in the area someplace. Mom didn't know exactly where. She had gone on a trip and was on her way back when the storm started."

"She's probably sitting in her car waiting out the storm," Martha said.

Nelson came into the room. "Trudy, I need to talk to you."

They walked into the breezeway, and Nelson said, "A woman called the station and said she was driving a horse trailer with a horse and doesn't want to stop. She said she's not far from home. She told them where she was according to her GPS and it sounds like she's right by here. Wanna get your cars going again?"

"Let's go."

Nelson got on his phone and they headed for the garage after grabbing coats, boots and gloves.

*****

"Come on! Where are you?" Trudy said, hugging her coat to her body as she sat in her car and honked the horn.

"I think I see something," Nelson said, pointing.

Trudy could barely make out headlights and honked rapidly. The snow slowed and they could now see the truck and trailer. She jumped out of her car and went to a garage door. Nelson ran out of the garage toward the pickup. It stopped and he went around to the driver's side. The woman opened her window.

"I'm so glad to see you. I thought there was a big white farm house there. And this smaller house didn't even show up on the map."

"The white house burnt down yesterday. This house is a new build so it probably wouldn't even show up," Nelson told her. "I need you to pull across the drive with the back of your trailer close to the open door on the right. We'll off load your horse into the garage."

The woman's mouth opened but nothing came out.

"What?" Nelson asked.

"Are you sure you want a horse in your garage?" she asked.

"Not my garage, but the owner thought it would be better to get the horse out of the trailer."

"How about my dog?" the woman asked.

"Yep. Him too. But let's get the horse and anything else you'll need out first, and then you can get your dog."

"Okay. If you say so."

Nelson went inside the garage and watched the truck pull laterally across the large concrete driveway.

"Stop!" he hollered. The truck stopped and the young woman jumped out and went to the trailer. Trudy met her there.

"Hi. I'm Trudy."

"I'm CJ Carter. Are you the owner?"

"Yes, I am. The winds are starting to whip up again. We'd better get him in before it gets worse."

CJ pulled a ramp out and down to rest on the cement. She then opened the back of the trailer and walked in. Nelson was standing on the other side of the open trailer door and Trudy went into the garage. CJ backed a gray dappled colt out and walked him into the garage.

"Hook him here." Trudy showed her a place where she kept her dogs sometimes when she went out. "Got food? I got water." She went to fill a bucket with water as CJ went back to the trailer.

Nelson and CJ came in with a bale of hay, a bucket of oats and a suitcase.

"Here's some water." Trudy set the bucket down. "Do you have everything?"

"Everything but my dog." CJ headed back out into the storm.

Trudy and Nelson stood looking at the beautiful horse when a black fluffy dog came bounding in and greeted them. CJ followed.

"Where do you want me to park my truck?"

Trudy loved the dog up. "Just leave it there. Is it turned off?"

CJ ran out into the snow again and returned a few minutes later. "Yep."

Trudy closed the garage doors. "I have a sofa sleeper for you to use tonight, CJ."

"I'm going in," Nelson said.

"Don't tell anyone. I don't want a crowd out here."

"Crowd?" CJ asked.

Nelson waved backwards as he headed in. "We have a few more stranded people staying the night."

"I have a sleeping bag. I'll just stay out here with the animals."

"I have a cot you can use." Trudy went to double doors on the far end of the garage. When she returned, she was pushing a roll-a-way.

"Thanks, Trudy. This will be good." CJ took the bed over to where she'd sleep.

"Why don't you come in and get something to eat and drink at least."

"I'd like that. Oh, and I need to call my folks. My phone died."

"You can use mine and plug your phone in on the work bench over there." Trudy pointed at a plug in.

"Oh shoot! My charger is in my truck."

"I have a charger you can use. Let's go get you something to eat."

*****

Trudy and CJ walked into the kitchen. Joy and Martha were sitting at the table talking.

Joy stood. "What's going on? Nelson wouldn't tell us."

"I'm sorry. I didn't mean for him not to tell you guys. We have a new guest, CJ Carter, her dog and a colt."

"The colt's for my little sister," CJ said.

"Speaking of little sister," Trudy started, "how's Icicle?"

"The group convinced her to go downstairs with them, but she's awfully quiet," Martha said.

CJ looked at Martha. "I know you."

"I sure hope so. You used to ride my bus," Martha said.

"Icicle! Gotta be my crazy little sister who wears flip flops in the winter."

Joy and Martha started laughing.

"Yep! That's her," Trudy said. "She was frozen by the time the kids got here."

"Oh my gosh! What happened?"

"The school bus slid off the road," Martha replied. "A deputy stopped to help and his squad car slid off the road too, so we all walked here."

"Your mom told her you were lost in the storm. They are all just sick with worry," Trudy said, as she handed her cell to CJ.

CJ took the phone. "Thanks."

"Call your folks and then I'll take you to Sue," Trudy said.

*****

Trudy got to the bottom of the stairs. "Icicle! Someone's here to see you."

Sue looked up and saw CJ. She screamed, "Cindi!" She raced around the sofa and threw herself into her big sister's arms.

Everyone clapped and cheered.

"I have Mom on the line." CJ put the phone to her ear. "Yes mom. We're okay. Hopefully we'll see you tomorrow. Love you too, Mom. Bye." CJ hung up and buried her face in her sister's hair. Nelson's phone rang and he answered it as he walked away. Trudy watched the kids interact joyfully and the dogs were being spoiled.

Nelson came up to Trudy, Joy and Martha. "The snow has stopped. The wind is settling down. Hopefully by sometime tomorrow the gravel road will be bladed and we can all chip in and shovel out."

"I have someone down the road to blade, but it depends on how deep it is. I don't know about you guys, but I'm going to go up to the front porch and look at the snow," Trudy said. She picked her little dog up from the back of the couch and headed upstairs with her golden retriever on her heels.

Joy had her little dog secure in her arms as they ascended the steps, followed by everyone else.

They looked at the tons of drifted snow from the warmth of Trudy's porch.

"Brrrr! Glad it's out there and we're in here," Joy said.

"Hot chocolate anyone?" Trudy said.

Everyone headed into the house except Sue, Deb and CJ. They went to the garage.

By ten the TVs were off. Nelson and the boys were downstairs, and Martha and the girls were upstairs. Joy and her dog snuggled under numerous blankets on the sofa in the family room.

*****

At seven the next morning, Trudy followed her dogs through her quiet house. A nightlight glowed at the kitchen counter. They made their way to the back to go out. When the dogs were done, she let them into the laundry room for breakfast, putting food in their dishes and filling their water bowls.

Still not quite awake, she walked up the hall and turned in to the butlers' pantry. She made a quick cup of coffee, stirred a mocha flavoring into it, and walked through to the kitchen. Joy, Martha, Nelson, CJ and the kids stood all around the kitchen island looking at her with big smiles on their faces. Trudy lowered the cup.

"What's wrong?" she asked, cautiously.

Sue and Deb held up a birthday cake, candles flickering on top. They set it on the counter. Trudy put her hand over her mouth. The kids on her left parted. Someone flipped a switch and the house glowed with Christmas lights and decorations.

Tears rolled down Trudy's cheeks. Joy and Martha stepped forward. Martha took Trudy's cup and Joy put her arm around her waist. Someone flipped another switch and the Christmas tree glowed!

"Best Christmas tree ever!" Trudy choked out.

The kids started to sing, 'Joy to the World,' and everyone joined in.

*****

By two p.m., because of the kids' hard work and her neighbor down the road, they were all dug out. A school van pulled in front of Trudy's house. After hugs and goodbyes, Martha and the kids headed out the front door. Waving, Trudy and Joy stood at the door with smiles on their faces.

"It's going to be a great Christmas this year," Trudy said. "This whole situation could have turned out so very bad. We were all very blessed."

"Yes, we were," Joy agreed.

The two women headed into the house, the dogs zipped by them. The house phone rang.

"I bet that's one of my daughters." Joy picked up the phone. "Hi, honey. We're all dug out. When are you coming?" she asked as she climbed the stairs to her room.

Trudy's cell rang and she looked at it. One of her grandsons. "Hi, sweetheart. I'm fine. You'll be here tomorrow? Terrific! I can't wait." Hanging up, she looked at the tree and smiled.

The doorbell rang and the dogs ran barking.

"Get back you guys." Trudy opened the front door and there stood…

"Jake. Anything wrong?"

"Nope. Just wanted to check and make sure everything was okay."

Trudy smiled.

AD Stein

The 7:47 a.m. Shuttle
By
~~M.L. Carr~~ A. Helvey

I've met Presidents. Famous baseball players like Andy Pafko, outfielder for the Milwaukee Braves. Ed Koch, Helen Thomas, J.J. Cale. And let's not forget Maria Tallchief, the world renowned ballerina. I operate the 7:47 a.m. shuttle every day except Tuesday. But, let me tell you how my need for speed led me to this terrific job.

*****

My brother and I were born into a family of Lutherans who rented small farms in Dallas County, Iowa, and both our parents worked two jobs to support us. Our last name is Miller, and because my mother thought Miller was such a common last name, she gave us prestigious first and middle names. "To distinguish you from the thousands of other Millers in this country," she told us when we were older. I am named after Franklin Roosevelt and my brother is named after Thomas Jefferson.

Tom and I live at Lake Shore Manor with ninety-two other "active seniors." The lake is really a pond with mallards and a few Canadian geese who brave the winter here in Iowa. Today is December third and Wanda, the activity director, has asked housekeeping to lug up the bins of Christmas decorations from storage. Our tradition is to gather in the Kirkwood Community Room to sing carols and help decorate the entire building.

It seems to me that every year Wanda's collection expands. It currently includes dozens of lighted trees, reindeer, Santa's, trains, bears that laugh, snow globes with Christmas scenes swirling in white glitter, elves that talk when you walk past them, plaques with joyous quotes, fake candles, and miles of garland festooned with pine cones and candy canes. Tom and I will be working in the west wing. We'll drape every door knob with a red satin ribbon holding a wooden plaque that says, 'Seasons Greetings', or 'HO HO HO'.

Wanda's mantra is "a busy senior is a happy senior," which accounts for the daily schedule of activities. We have bingo every week, trips to Walmart and the Safeway grocery store, and entertainment such as Arthur and His Amazing Accordion. On Tuesdays and Thursdays it's sing-a-long in the lobby at two o'clock with Juney Toon. Not her real name I'll bet. On Mondays and Fridays it's senior exercises or aerobics, in case I want to learn the triple axel for the next Ice Follies. Of course I never miss the big birthday party bash for everyone born that month. At seventy-nine years old, I can finally eat all the ice cream I want.

On Wednesdays the schedule is hectic. We play poker and bingo in the morning, and then at 2:00 pm we have Men's Group. It's not AA or group therapy where we talk about our feelings or sentimental stuff. No, we spend the first ten minutes discussing health issues such as hip pain, new meds and their effects, or the big one, incontinence. The next ten minutes we share information about our loved ones or special moments with other residents. The next ten minutes we tell lies about our youth where embellishment is encouraged. Then we vote on who told the best lie. The winner presents the "topic of the week" for the remaining thirty minutes. Afterwards Tom announces to everyone, "I think it's Pabst o'clock," and we relocate to Bruce's Duces.

Last week I told the best lie so it was my turn to share a story. I decided to tell the group about the acquisition of my new bike when I was eight.

I was always compelled to to go faster and higher than the rest of the kids on Forest Avenue, whether it was roller skating or flying kites. School was out for the third grade in June. I started dropping strong hints, and talked about nothing else, except wanting a new bicycle for my eighth birthday in July. I was probably the last boy at Madison Elementary to own a bicycle with training wheels. I shared the bike with my brother Tom, who was only six. When my dad took me with him on a trip to Sears in Des Moines to look at new lawnmowers, I spotted my new dream bike. It was dark blue with wide black tires and had streamers of silver and metallic blue hanging from the handles. Ted Hanson didn't even have anything that cool. I pictured myself skyrocketing down Forest Avenue while the other guys –Buzzy, Tiny and Ted watched in awe as my Schwinn and I gained speed before curving down Pine Ridge Road to Patsy Anderson's house.

Mom and Dad bought that bike for my birthday. I was both thrilled and scared to try it out. Dad said I needed to learn hand signals for left and right turns. He told me, "It's a part of being a courteous driver now that you have graduated to a big boy's bike."

"Geez, you mean I have to take my hand off the handle bar while traveling at one hundred miles per hour to signal to someone behind me, even if there is no one behind me?" These adult rules didn't make much sense.

Around the third week of putting miles on my new bike, Patsy Anderson was out on her porch swing one Wednesday afternoon. Tiny and Ted were in the garage next door working on their Cub Scout project. Big Blue (that's what I named my bike) and I were speeding down Forest when I decided to impress everyone with my new abilities. I rounded the corner at Pine Ridge and yelled, "Look, no hands!"

I took both hands off the handles and held them in the air up over my head, balancing carefully for a few yards. I further impressed them by clinching my eyes shut and yelling, "Look, no eyes!"

The whole street was watching me. I felt the evening air breezing through my wet hair and pulling my tee shirt away from my body. Perspiration evaporated off my palms as they faced toward the pink and blue sky. I felt exhilarated and wild. I was thinking Tiny and Ted probably thought I was cool. I was certain Patsy thought I was daring and wonderful.

Suddenly, I heard them yelling, their voices garbled, one on top the other and difficult to understand. Bike…car…stop…turn…

I catapulted through the air and landed hard, sprawled out on the cement with bloody elbows and torn knees. Mr. Anderson charged out of his garage and ran to help me. My bicycle tire had wedged between the front bumper and left fender of his parked Chrysler Imperial. The front tire of Big Blue was headed west, while the handle bars were headed south.

I lay moaning on the concrete, agonizing more about what Patsy thought than how much I hurt. I was afraid of Mr. Anderson and worried about the damage I'd done to his car. I was double scared about what my dad was going to do to me since I did not "operate the bike in a safe and prudent manner" as he had warned me.

But the elation and freedom of closing my eyes and coasting, coasting almost on air with a purple sky on my palms, never left me. The adventurous spirit within me was ignited.

Group adjourned ten minutes late on December third, so all of us decided to take the shuttle van to Safeway. Instead of shopping, we detoured our walkers and scooters next door to Bruce's Duces for a cold draft beer and constructed more lies.

The next week, December tenth, Men's Group met again at two o'clock. Dwayne complained that Conrad talked too much about his hip giving him spasms. Larry said George shouldn't use the same big lie he used a month ago. George said he didn't, but none of the rest of us could remember. After ten minutes of bickering, Thomas said, "Why don't we skip the big lie segment and ask Franklin to finish his driving story." Everyone finally agreed on something.

*****

My folks moved to the country, near Ida Grove, when I was twelve. Dad worked for Pioneer Seed Corn and was promoted to sales manager for the northern part of Iowa and southern Minnesota. Ida Grove was okay. It had an airplane show once a year and a neat theme park with moats, castles, and stuff like that.

Ida Grove had a golf course where my dad learned to play golf so he could entertain clients when he traveled. The best part is he let me take golf lessons. On Sundays after church and lunch, we'd go out for nine holes. I liked golfing with dad because Pete Peterson, the funeral director, and his son Adam made up our foursome. Adam knew a lot about anatomy and I took a serious interest in the subject after I met his sister, Merrilea. She was an excellent basketball player and had her own horse named Zeus. Learning to ride a horse with Merrilea giving me instructions was more fun than learning to ride the bicycle.

Mom and dad had an acreage outside of town about six miles. Dad didn't really farm, but we had a few pigs in a small lot next to the well house for my 4H project, and five calves in the pasture beyond the garden. Thomas showed the calves and usually took home a few ribbons. Mom grew most of our vegetables, some of which she entered in the State Fair in Des Moines. By this time, I was on to bigger and better interests like cars.

For dad's thirty-sixth birthday, mom bought him a red Farm All tractor from the neighbor for two hundred and fifty dollars.

Dad wanted to plow up the lower pasture and plant millet for the birds and pheasants and corn for the livestock, but Dad's new promotion kept him on the road most of the spring, which left me in charge of that acreage.

Mom said the thistles were so bad that we had to keep them plowed under. I learned to drive the tractor with help from our neighbor, Dallas. He instructed me on how to put in the clutch, which was the left pedal, and how to apply the brakes when necessary. There was a left and right wheel brake. After the clutch was in, I was supposed to push the gear shift forward into first. The tractor had five forward gears, which was a lot of learning considering my bike had no gears at all. I was somewhat exasperated trying to operate that huge tractor when Dallas reignited my interest by saying, "Once you've mastered the Farm All, the Corvette will be a piece of cake."

During that summer and the next, I did master making turns and straight rows. I learned about refueling, changing oil, checking the hydraulic hitch and when to come in for a drink of lemonade after too much sun. I digested the importance of nutrition with ham sandwiches and cole slaw lunches in the pasture as I stretched out on a patch of violets, and I learned about working until late into the night when a storm was in the forecast. But, the best thing I figured out was that Merrilea could ride next to me in the cab. As long as I kept the tractor moving, Mom didn't ask me to come in for supper and Merrilea sat close to me and squeezed my hand.

In October after a really wet summer, I was picking the last few acres of corn late into the day. It was about ten o'clock and there was a harvest moon, one of those over-sized orange spheres in the crisp black sky. I let my tired arms slump around the steering wheel and let the tractor run forward on its own power for the rest of the row. It was going about six miles per hour, very slow and chugging. Occasionally when I dozed off, I lurched it back in line just as we reached the end of the row. There was stillness. No breeze rushing, no exhilaration. Only the sound of corn stripped off its stalk and the kernels grinding up the conveyer belt…a termination of life. Even though my arms were resting on the wheel, I felt powerless. The tractor owned the triumphant victory of bringing in the crops, or turning over the soil, something that would have taken me all summer to do with my back and a shovel. I realized how unimportant I was in the whole scheme of things. I was only an instrument in getting the job done.

*****

Group adjourned late again the next week, but there was still time to help Wanda stuff stockings with candy for the children who came to visit over the holiday. The local high school brought a bus load of students to perform traditional Christmas songs while Juney Toon accompanied them on the piano. Wanda went all out again this year, and with the help of staff and us active seniors, we decorated twelve trees that adorned every wing and gathering place. One tree was designated for the daycare center downtown where most of the children who went there lived in poverty. The ladies made knitted hats, mittens and scarves to pin on the tree. Old men like Larry, George and me, we took the easy route and clipped five dollar bills to the tree for the children. The kids were scheduled to attend the following Wednesday, December sixteenth. We discussed that after the Men's Group meeting, we'd all go and welcome our little guests.

The December sixteenth meeting of the Men's Group was interrupted when the electricity went off. Evidently, all those twinkling lights and multiple trains running on elaborate tracks caused a power failure. Then the cookies and brownies baking in the kitchen set off a smoke alarm that blared like a fire siren. We had a choice - wait it out in the heated garage or move the Men's Group to Bruce's Duces. The vote was unanimous. In route on the shuttle, all of the men decided that I should continue my saga about learning to drive. Conrad ordered a round of Pabsts Blue

Ribbons for everyone and we passed around the plastic basket of peanuts.

*****

When I turned sixteen, I did not get a Corvette. My dad and I had been working on a red Thunderbird convertible for about a year. It had a blown motor and it had been rolled. Dad thought we could rebuild it into a really serviceable vehicle. He also thought it would be fun if we worked on the car together. I had a job at the HyVee grocery store and needed a car to get around on my own. It was funny how close to my birthday he got that car running. In later years I realized he planned it that way all along. Dad drove me to take the driver's test. Naturally I passed since I already knew how to drive the tractor and had taken Driver's Ed. Dad wanted me to take him for a ride in the convertible. How corny, my dad riding with me with the top down. I had thoughts of Merrilea, but dad said he wanted to be first to ride in The Bird.

"Don't forget to turn on the signal before you turn…even if there is no car in sight. You just never know if something is around the corner…remember the bicycle."

"Always watch for the oil light. Change that oil every three thousand miles or three months."

"This car has seat belts for a reason. Always make sure you and your passenger have your seat belts on, even if you're just going to HyVee. Remember, most accidents happen within two miles of your home."

I don't know if Dad ever knew that later that night I kissed Merrilea in that car and asked her to go steady. When she said yes, I wasn't sure if I should signal left or right, roll up the windows, honk the horn, or tie a white handkerchief to the antenna. I do recall speeding down Hawthorn Avenue, honking at my friends, driving around the town square yelling, "Merrilea and I are going steady." I stood up with my foot on the accelerator and raised up my arms toward the sky and screamed over the sound of the radio,

"Merrilea, take over for a second," and she steered around the corners of the square.

I wanted to feel the hot July night air against my nervous palms, feel the grit of black dirt hitting my chest and blotching my white tee shirt. My ears loved the sound of tires squealing against the pavement and I remember the smell of Merrilea's Passion Perfume wafting across my face. I wanted this night to never end.

It was after midnight when I drove her home, well past her curfew and way into big trouble with her dad, who was sitting with her mother on the front porch swing. About two hundred feet before I pulled The Bird into her driveway, I turned on the right signal. After all, I had learned the rules of driving.

*****

The December twenty-third Men's Group meeting came together in the afternoon. All of the guys decided to forego the usual business meeting and get down to the rest of my story. I was feeling pretty accommodating. Who doesn't like being the center of attention?

By the time we celebrated our seventh wedding anniversary, Merrilea and I had a family of four – Mandy, Sandy, Ricky and Mickey. We moved to Spirit Lake where I had a job with Pioneer. My territory was similar to the one my father had. Merrilea had gone to Iowa Beauty College after we graduated from high school and she had her own business. She attended all of the children's school plays, softball games and piano recitals. I taught my kids how to ride bicycles, paddle canoes and drive a car just like my dad taught me. None of them had a Thunderbird convertible though. Instead, I bought them more practical cars like a Ford Escort and one of those Subaru station wagons we used to haul chicken feed and plywood.

I think it was around our thirtieth wedding anniversary when Merrilea and I decided not to buy each other a gift. Instead, we wanted to buy something the whole family could enjoy. We chose a candy-apple red cabin cruiser, a Bayliner 3870 with two state rooms and air conditioning that we found at a marina near Spirit Lake. Merrilea loved the two bathrooms and small galley kitchen with refrigerator. Our only granddaughter wanted us to name the boat Tinkerbell, after I told her most boats have girl names. But she was ecstatic when we named it after her, Shelley's Star, because after all, Tinkerbell did have a magic wand with a star.

I had never operated a boat before and wanted to learn fast so we could have our children and grandchildren come to the lakes for the July 4th weekend. My friend, Keith, went with me the first time we put Shelley's Star in the water and he taught me the basics of steering, turning, how to pull a skier, and docking etiquette. I pushed the throttle forward and the boat responded instantly with a fast thrust ahead. It steered quickly and took the turns tight. To back off on the speed, I just pulled back on the throttle. So simple. No gears, no brakes, no shifting.

A few weeks after we purchased the Star, I signed up for a boating safety course offered by the DNR and took Ricky and Merrilea with me. Anyone who operated my boat needed to understand the rules first.

We boated all day July 4th, docking occasionally for ice and more sun block for the grandkids. I loved the feeling of power from the cruiser, the feeling of exhilaration as the wind pulled the hair away from my head. I sped through the waves, crashing them into pieces as I broke the whitecaps.

As the day waned and the last of the crimson sun seared my face, the sky filled with shooting streaks of salmon and blue over the lake. I couldn't have been happier. I watched the waves move in and out, heaving rocks, sand and froth onto the shore. Soon we were in darkness and the sky and lake melted together in layers of lavender and grey. I liked the sound of pelicans, night frogs and fish splashing into the algae. The lake mist enveloped me and my family into a cocoon of closeness. There were a few boats left on the lake after the fireworks when I turned back toward the docks, skimming the black water at moderate speed. I couldn't resist the urge and let go of the steering wheel for only a few moments, allowing the boat to glide across the glassy water by itself…silent, secret. I stretched my arms up to the sky to feel the murky heavy mist and listened to the churning water around me. The sounds of the night and their melodic harmonies were hypnotic to me. I felt at peace. I did not hear the boat motor. I did not hear the grandchildren. I only heard the only the song of the bugs and the rasp of waves against the bow.

Merrilea died of cancer five years ago, a suitable time to die. She was too tired and too frail. The kids and grandchildren were married and off to college. She had made about as many quilts as her eyes and hands would permit. No more grape jelly or apple crumb cake entries at the Dickinson County Fair. No more boating at the lake and no more sitting in the Thunderbird that was stored in the barn. I finally gave it to one of the grandkids in spite of his moaning that he wanted something more modern with electric windows and cruise control.

With my Merrilea gone, I eventually gave up. I could not keep up the house, nor the acreage. My health failed with diabetes and heart disease. I lost my beloved wife, my garden, the picnic table outside the kitchen, my car privileges. I could no longer meet my old customers and friends at the Cascade Café to discuss politics and recent obituaries. The children arranged for me to live at Lake Shore Manor and, well, you know the rest of the story.

*****

About a year ago, my legs gave out when I fell in the shower and hurt my back. The doctor told me I had to learn to operate a wheelchair if I wanted to get around. At my age, no one should have to learn something new, least of all a turtle paced wheelchair. My need for speed was indefinitely suspended. I hated the thought of it. The nurse told me maneuvering the wheelchair was as easy as falling off a log. I've done that and it hurt.

There were a few kerfuffles with the automatic front doors, several hiccup moments with the elevator door, a collision with Mrs. Newman's bullet speed scooter and, I was reminded more than once, not to attempt the shuttle bus ramp without assistance from the burly driver, Rex. Once I mastered the wheelchair, which was similar to the Farm All in terms of speed, I could roll through the salad bar in no time, zoom into bingo and charge into Physical Therapy in a matter of minutes. PT, or Pain and Torture as I call it, is supposed to help me with range of motion and strengthen my muscles…joke.

For Christmas Day I reserved the Anchor Room for our family gathering. Mandy, Sandy, Ricky and Mickey, along with their families, brought gifts and covered dishes for our dinner. We ate bourbon-glazed ham balls, barbecued chicken wings, Chinese salad with sesame dressing, potato wedges with sour cream and bacon, apple salad, tomatoes and mozzarella, roasted red beets with goat cheese and arugula, sweet potatoes with brown sugar and slabs of butter, mashed potatoes and golden chicken gravy, cheddar biscuits, green bean casserole with crispy French-fried onion ring topping, peach pie in a shortbread crust with whipped cream, pumpkin cheesecake, Sandy's peanut brittle, Ricky's fudge brownies with peppermint and chocolate frosting, and Mandy's Jello Surprise, just like her mother used to make.

My heart was joyous as I sang traditional Christmas songs with the grandchildren. We took selfies and old-fashioned photos with my Cannon single lens reflex, a hot find at K-Mart years ago. I told stories about the long ago days on the farm in Ida Grove and how I learned to drive The Bird. After about twenty minutes, the grandkids were bored and turned to texting their friends and taking selfies with me in the background. I'm certain the caption read Gramps or Grumpy. My daughters cleaned up the Anchor Room, stuffed all the gift wrap and tissue into a black plastic bag and then poured glasses of Jim Beam over ice for the men as they watched Oklahoma City Thunder versus the Miami Heat on the big screen television. This was a Christmas to remember.

Back at my "spacious unit overlooking the lake," I was tired. I hobbled out of the wheelchair and settled in the recliner to watch the prerecorded episode of Jeopardy. I felt truly blessed for my children, grandchildren, parents and my lovely Merrilea.

Early the next morning, about 7:30 a.m., a cardinal's song woke me. Was it spring? I didn't think so, and I went into the bathroom for a piss and a shave. While I washed my face with one of those "collagen buffering sponges" that I picked up at Thompson's Pharmacy on sample day, I definitely heard the sound of a cardinal and a tractor. How unusual…wrong time of the year I thought, but at my age…maybe I was just confused.

I put on the burgundy cardigan sweater Shelley gave me for Christmas and decided I'd patrol the hallway for anything unusual. My wheelchair rolled past Tom's apartment and down toward the emergency exit that had a window in the door. I heard a tractor outside plowing, churning up the soil, chugging through the field, preparing for planting…new crops, new harvest. I rose from the wheelchair to get a better look out of the emergency exit door window, but it was fogged up.

Maybe it was spring and the farmers were spraying chemicals in the fields today. Maybe it was a snow storm like Wanda told me last night. I leaned against the exit door to get a better look. The door swung open, the emergency alarm filled the hall, and I pitched forward out the door into a bank of snow.

In front of me, a beautiful garden with pink and cream blooming roses spread across the snowy lawn. A lovely stone fountain, on my left, was filled with bluebirds and cherubs darting in and out of the foam as it cascaded down all three tiers. A hummingbird dove through the mist and hovered in front of me. I lay there, awed in silence. I was perplexed and astonished. Through a powdery cloud I saw a familiar face wreathed in a big smile. It was Merrilea.

"Hello Cupcake, I've missed you," she said. She motioned me over.

She sat in the back bench of a three-wheeled chariot wearing the turquoise poodle skirt and pink lipstick she wore to our first dance at the Surf Ballroom. The tall man who held the reins looked familiar. He had a kind face and wore a long white plush robe similar to the ones they gave residents of Walnut Park Senior Living, the expensive place across town.

"Hello Franklin, I'm J.C. and I'm going to teach you how to drive this chariot. Hop on in," he said as he extended his hand to help me climb aboard.

"J.C.? Did your mother name you after Jimmy Carter, the President, like my mom named me?"

"Yes, you could say that."

He put a misty arm around me and handed me the reins.

"Where are we going? What is this? I'm not sure what to do." Even after all these years of learning to drive cars, boats, tractors and a wheelchair, I was afraid I wouldn't operate the chariot correctly.

"This is the 7:47 a.m. shuttle, affectionately called the Rocket. I think you'll like it. The speed is amazing."

The six platinum-colored horses were twice the size of any horse I'd ever seen. Their muscles twitched and shimmered as they pounded the ground with their silver hooves, anxious to get moving.

"Are you ready to put this in top gear?" J.C. asked.

Astonished, I said, "No, I've never even seen the manual."

"You won't need a manual and you don't need to use hand signals. Just snap the reins and tell the stallions where you want to go. Up, down, forward, backward, sideways, circles, fast or slow."

"Do I need a seatbelt?" I asked.

"No, not today."

I gently flicked the reins and shouted, "Giddy up."

We hit lift-off and accelerated above the earth in a second.

The sky was filled with silver streamers and long curly ribbons of blue and gold. White doves swooped around us and snow, scented like lilacs, fell upon us. The howling wind tossed the horses' long, flowing manes into the icy crystals of light. The cold air pulled my hair straight. I let go of the reins, turned my tired palms toward the pink and blue sky and squeezed my eyes shut. I inhaled my last breath.

"Look, no hands!"

Silver Bells
By
C. Deanne Rowe

"And now, the most requested song of this holiday season." Sloane Thomas flipped the mute switch and placed her headphones on the desk.

"Being a DJ this time of year can almost make you hate Christmas," she said to Sherri. "As much as I love Christmas music, if I have to listen to that song one more time, I'll scream. Thank goodness Christmas will be over in a few weeks."

"Here's a package that just came for you."

Sherri placed the box on the desk in front of Sloane. Checking for any hint of where the package might have come from, all Sloane could see was her name and the address of the radio station on a printed label.

"Who delivered this? Can't be UPS, Federal Express or even the Postal Service. There's no postage or markings."

"It was a local delivery service if that helps. I didn't recognize the name but I had to sign for it. I can go look and see if there is anything else that might tell you who it's from, or you can open it and see if there's a card or something."

"That's why they pay you the big bucks, Sherri." Sloane smiled. "Why don't I open it?"

Sloane grabbed a letter opener laying on her desk and split the tape on the cardboard box. From the pile of bubble wrap inside the box, she removed a round silver metal container and opened the top of it.

"I can't believe this. No one would know."

"Know what?" Sherri asked.

"About these Christmas cookies." Sloan held up one of the cookies, inspecting it in the light. "My grandmother and I would make cookies exactly like this every Christmas."

"They look like just decorated sugar cookies. What's so special about them that makes you think of your grandmother? A lot of people make decorated cookies every Christmas."

"They're all silver bells. Grandmother had a lot of different Christmas cookie cutters to use but we only made the silver bells."

"You're sure they're all silver bells?" Sherri leaned over to take a closer look in the container of cookies. "You're right. They're all silver bells. Maybe your grandmother sent them to you."

"I wish that was true, but it's impossible," Sloane replied.

"Why?" Sherri asked.

"My grandmother has been in a coma for the past six months. I don't believe it would be possible for her to make Christmas cookies and have them delivered to me in her condition."

"That's probably true," Sherri replied. "There has to be an explanation. Or else it's a big coincidence."

"If it's a big coincidence, then it's kinda creepy. Don't you agree?"

Sloane closed the lid of the container and placed it back in the box. She'd worry about it later. Right now the Christmas song she was playing was about over. She had to get back on the air.

*****

Sloane made an attempt to apply her makeup so it hid her lack of sleep. She wasn't having much success. Worrying about where the cookies could have come from had caused her to toss and turn all night. The dark circles under her eyes would give her away.

Pouring a travel cup full of coffee, Sloane picked up her purse and tote bag. Before she could leave, there was a knock on her front door. When she opened it, her next door neighbor was smiling and holding a brown cardboard box a little smaller than the one which was delivered to the radio station yesterday. He was nicely dressed and looked as if he was in a hurry to leave for work.

"Good morning, Sloane. A delivery service left this for you yesterday. I signed for it but completely forgot to deliver it to you. Sorry, but I've got to run. I'm already late."

"Thank you," was all Sloane managed to get out before her neighbor disappeared into the parking lot.

"This is definitely getting very creepy."

Sloane closed her front door and placed the box on the kitchen cabinet along with her coffee mug, purse and bag. She searched through her kitchen drawers for a knife to open the package. Inside, buried in a pile of bubble wrap, was another round metal container. It was silver just like the last one, but smaller.

"What, more cookies?"

Opening the container, Sloane couldn't believe what she saw. Instead of decorated sugar cookies shaped like silver bells, this container was full of silver bell Christmas ornaments, all different shapes and sizes.

"What is going on, Grandmother?" Sloane closed her eyes and whispered, hoping somehow an answer would magically come. What came instead were memories of how her grandmother would always put lights and garland on her Christmas tree, but the only ornaments she would use were silver bells.

Sloane put the lid on the container and inspected this box for any hint of where or who it might be from. There was nothing, just like the box delivered to the radio station yesterday. She picked up her coffee, purse and tote bag and left for work, not able to get the ornaments off her mind the entire drive.

After arriving at work, Sloane took a minute before she had to go on the air to call the nursing home and make sure there was no change in her grandmother's condition.

"She is still in a coma. None of her vitals have changed in the past few days," the nurse explained.

"She hasn't been awake at all?" Sloane asked.

"No, Sloane. Your grandmother's condition has stayed the same. We'll certainly call you if that changes."

"What about visitors? Has she had any visitors the past few weeks?"

"No visitors at all. Would you like a call if someone does come for a visit?"

"Yes, please. That would be great. Thank you."

Sloane knew there was no one other than her grandfather, her family and one of her closest childhood friends who knew about the silver bells. Her grandfather had passed away over ten years ago. There were very few family members left, and she hadn't seen or talked to her childhood friend since he moved away in grade school and broke her heart. Sloane had guarded her grandmother's story as if it was their special secret. It made her feel closer to her grandmother, having this secret only a special few knew.

Sloane had asked her grandmother every Christmas to tell her the story of how her grandfather had proposed by tying her engagement ring to a silver bell Christmas ornament and hanging it on her parent's Christmas tree. Every year after they were married, he would give her a new Christmas ornament in the shape of a silver bell.

Celebrating Christmas this year was going to be especially hard now that her grandmother was in a coma. Her parents being killed in a car accident on Christmas Eve when she was in college made celebrating hard, but at least she had her grandmother. With her grandmother in a coma, Sloane knew it would be difficult to find any joy in Christmas. The appearance of these strange packages was one of the meanest pranks she could think of. Who could possibly be behind it?

Finishing her shift, Sloane breathed a sigh of relief that no other package had been delivered today. She wasn't sure she could handle another surprise. The last two had given her enough to think about.

As she got closer to her car, Sloane noticed an envelope underneath her windshield wiper on the driver's side. She looked around before she took the envelope out from under the wiper, then slipped it in her bag and climbed into her car, quickly locking the doors.

She had read stories about people putting notes or money under the wipers of a parked car. Usually the driver didn't notice it until he or she had already opened the car door. The thieves would then steal the car when the driver was removing whatever was under the wiper. Sloane started her car, deciding she would wait until she was home to read the note.

Whoever was behind these things knew where she worked, where she lived and what car she drove. Sloane didn't like what was happening at all.

Paying close attention to any strangers who might be milling around in the parking lot of her apartment building, Sloane felt sure no one had followed her home. She knew she would be safe walking the short distance to her apartment, but she didn't feel safe under she had her apartment door locked behind her.

Then, after carefully opening the envelope she had removed from her tote bag, Sloane pulled out a handmade Christmas card shaped like a bell and covered in silver glitter. The card looked exactly like the ones she and her grandmother made and sent out every year with their Christmas letter enclosed. She was a little hesitant to open the card, but she noticed a folded piece of paper tucked inside. It was sealed with a little silver bells sticker. Maybe it held a clue to who was behind all of these surprises.

Sloane,

I know you will feel alone this Christmas. I also know how hard it has been for you to find any joy this time of year since your parents passed so close to Christmas. I'm sorry I can't physically be with you to share another Christmas. I will still be with you in spirit. Please don't let your sorrow and loss overpower all the wonders of the Christmas season. Remember the meaning of the season. The birth of Jesus Christ. Lean on him and let him help you through these tough times. I want you to know you will never be alone. Your parents and I will be watching over you and bringing the right people into your life to love and cherish you as we do. Keep all the memories we shared close to your heart. Please don't be so full of sorrow that you forget to make memories of your own. I love you.

Grandmother

Sloane felt tears stream down her cheeks. She folded the letter and carefully placed it back in the envelope, then picked up her cell phone and called the nursing home.

"This is Sloane Thomas. I'm calling to check on my grandmother."

"We were getting ready to call you. Your grandmother passed away only a few short minutes ago. She went peacefully in her sleep. I'm so sorry, Ms. Thomas."

Sloane couldn't say anything. Her grandmother was gone. Her mind was spinning in different directions with so many different thoughts. After reading the letter that mysteriously appeared on her car windshield, she wasn't sure how any of the things which had happened in the past few days could be explained.

Right now all Sloane knew was she needed to be with her grandmother. She couldn't give these strange things which were happening any more time or thought. She not only had to make it through another Christmas, but now she had to say her goodbyes to her grandmother.

*****

Sloane was relieved she was able to make it possible for her grandmother's funeral to be held two days before Christmas. Her grandmother had already made most of the funeral arrangements several years ago. When her grandfather passed away, Sloane remembered her grandmother telling her many times how she didn't want the family to concern themselves with making arrangements for her funeral when she passed. She wanted to get them out of the way so she didn't burden anyone.

Sloane couldn't help but wonder how long ago her grandmother had written the letter that had been placed in the silver bell Christmas card she received. She had not only lost her parents on Christmas Eve but now she was burying her grandmother two days before Christmas.

Sloane remembered how Christmas used to be a time of family celebrations. It had now become a somber time for her. There was nothing left for her to celebrate and no one left to celebrate with.

All that was left for Sloane to do was notify anyone close to grandmother about her service. There were only a handful of distant family members and friends left. Most of their relatives had already passed. She didn't anticipate very many people attending at all.

She submitted an obituary to the local newspaper. Her grandmother had lived in the same city since she was born, so Sloane was hoping anyone that knew her would read it and attend the funeral.

When she arrived at the church, the parking lot was fairly empty except for a bus from the nursing home where her grandmother had spent the past few years of her life. The staff must have provided transportation for whoever was able to attend.

Walking through the front doors of the church, Sloane made her way to the Sanctuary. She spotted her grandmother's casket placed in front of the pulpit. A spray of her grandmother's favorite flowers, carnations and roses, covered the top. She knew there wouldn't be a lot of people attending the service, but Sloane had wanted to make sure everything was beautiful for her grandmother, and it was.

She found a seat on the front pew after stopping to say hello to several of the women she recognized from the nursing home. Closing her eyes, Sloane began silently talking to her grandmother. Thanking her for all the times she had been there for her before and after her parents had passed. Letting her know how much she would miss her smile and kind heart. Her thoughts were interrupted by a male voice coming from behind her.

"Sloane."

She opened her eyes and turned around to look in a familiar face she hadn't seen in such a long time.

"I'm sorry to hear about Grandmother Thomas."

"Michael?"

Sloane couldn't believe he was here. She hadn't seen him in so many years. The last time was when she was twelve. With tears streaming down her cheeks, she had watched him drive off in his family's loaded-down automobile. She was sure her heart was breaking. They faithfully wrote letters at first but then they stopped a few years after he moved away.

Sloane remembered hearing that Michael's parents had moved back to town to be close to family but he didn't come with them because he was away attending college. Now he was standing close enough for her to reach out and touch. He hadn't changed much at all. The years they were apart had been good to him. He was as handsome a man as Sloane remembered him being as a boy.

"I came back to visit my parents for Christmas. I read your grandmother's obituary in the paper." Michael took a seat next to her in the pew. "I also learned about your parents. I'm so sorry for everything and that I wasn't here for you."

"I wish you could have been here but I understood. It had been a long time since we had seen each other or even talked. I couldn't have expected you to take time out of your life. I did wonder if you had forgotten me."

"How could I forget you?" Michael asked. "You are the best friend I've ever had. Even when we were apart, I still thought of you. I hope you can forgive me for not being here. That's why I didn't even think about saying no when I received your grandmother's letter."

"What letter?" Sloane asked.

"The letter she sent to my parents and they forwarded to me asking for a few favors. I didn't even need to know why. I just did what she asked."

"What did she ask you to do?" Sloane was confused. She didn't remember her grandmother mentioning she had written a letter to Michael. They had stopped talking about him because her grandmother knew how much it hurt for her to think about him.

"Have you received some strange gifts the past few days?" Michael asked.

Sloane thought back to the tin of cookies, the Christmas ornaments and the card left on her windshield.

"Yes. I have. How did you know?"

"Because I sent them."

"You sent them?" Sloane asked.

"Let me try and explain. In the letter I received from your grandmother, she asked me to send you silver bell Christmas cookies. I have to admit my mother helped me make them. Also an assortment of silver bell Christmas ornaments, and then to give you a sealed letter she had written to you enclosed in a Christmas card. She gave me specific instructions, explaining how her health was failing. She couldn't do these things herself but she wanted to make sure your Christmas was full of memories. I was happy to fulfill her requests."

"Wait. You said you got her letter a few weeks ago?" Sloane asked.

"Yes. My parents received her letter in the mail a few weeks ago and my mother called me, read it to me and then mailed it."

"That's not possible, Michael."

"Why? I wouldn't joke about something like this, Sloane. I know how close you and your grandmother were."

"It's not possible because Grandmother was in a coma for the past six months. She was not able to communicate in any way, much less write a letter to you."

Sloane and Michael sat next to each other in silence until the service began. Michael comforted Sloane by holding her hand during the service. Not understanding what was happening, Sloane remembered her grandmother's letter telling her she wouldn't be alone and that she would bring people into her life to love and cherish her as much as she did. She knew her grandmother had brought her and Michael back together, two long lost friends who needed each other now more than ever before.

*****

Sloane smiled as she heard her favorite Christmas song, Silver Bells, begin playing on the radio. She couldn't help but think of her grandmother. It was hard for Sloane to believe it had been a year since her grandmother passed. Even though it had been a hard year, a lot had happened. She and Michael had become close again. He had moved back home so they were able to spend more time together, catching up on everything they had missed the years they were apart.

Taking time to pick out the perfect present for Michael, Sloane couldn't wait until he arrived so they could exchange gifts. They had planned to spend this Christmas Eve together for the past year. Michael knew how hard Christmas time was for Sloane. He had told her many times he wanted them to make new memories so this time of the year wouldn't be so difficult for her. Sloane knew Michael coming back into her life was a gift from her grandmother, something she still wasn't sure how her grandmother had managed to arrange. But it didn't matter anymore how she had managed. All that mattered was she had, and Michael was a wonderful part of Sloane's life again.

Sloane glanced around the apartment, making sure everything was perfect. She had made Michael's favorite dinner and planned to serve her favorite wine, a combination which should be pleasing for both of them. Sloane wanted just the two of them to celebrate Christmas tonight. This weekend would be a family celebration with Michael and his family.

She took one quick glance in the mirror before she answered the knock on her front door.

"You look beautiful." Michael gave her a hug as he walked through the door. "Merry Christmas."

"Merry Christmas to you," Sloane replied taking the present Michael handed her.

"I hope you like it."

"I'm sure I will."

Sloane placed the present under the tree beside her gift to him.

"Are you hungry?" she asked Michael. "I made roasted chicken with vegetables. I also have a nice salad and some decorated sugar cookies for dessert."

"My favorite dinner. I can almost bet the cookies are silver bells. Am I right?"

"Of course." Sloane smiled. "I thought about making trees, snowmen and a few Santa Clauses, but it didn't seem right. Maybe next year."

"What do you say we open presents before we eat dinner?"

Sloane could see the excitement in Michael's eyes. He still had the same expression she remembered when they had exchanged presents as children. She was thankful Michael had managed to bring back some Christmas joy for her.

"I think that's a great idea."

Sloane picked up both presents from under the tree and placed them on the table, then took a seat next to Michael on the couch.

"Why don't you open your present first?" Michael said.

Carefully ripping the paper, Sloane opened the package to find a wooden hand-carved jewelry box.

"It's beautiful. I love it, Michael."

"I hoped you would. Open the top."

Sloane did what Michael asked only to hear it begin to play her favorite Christmas carol, Silver Bells.

"Oh, Michael. I don't know what to say."

Tears began to roll down Sloane's cheeks as she lifted the silver bell Christmas ornament from the jewelry box. Tied to the top of the ornament was a princess cut engagement ring.

"Say yes, you'll marry me. I love you, Sloane. I always have."

Sloane had to take a breath before answering. Memories of her grandmother and grandfather ran through her mind. She knew she loved Michael and he had managed to help her make wonderful new Christmas memories of her own, just like her grandmother had asked her to do.

"Yes, Michael. Of course, I'll marry you. I love you too."

Michael untied the ring from the top of the ornament and placed it on Sloane's finger.

"Now, let's hang the first of many ornaments on the Christmas tree."

It had been a long time coming, but Sloane couldn't think of any other time of the year which meant as much to her as Christmas.

Jingles Gets the Job Done
by
Amara Clay

"Girl are you all right?"

Claire's voice sounded far away. Dana lay on the ground, dazed and confused. Two large hands checked her head for cuts, and a soft, low voice asked, "Miss, are you all right?" before saying over his shoulder to his coworker, "Get kit number two out of the truck for me, please."

"Will she be okay, Mr...."

"It's Sandoval but call me Marco," the EMT said. "I'm just going to check your friend out and make sure she's all right. She has a pretty good bump on her head. We'll need to take her to the emergency room. Correct me if I'm wrong but this is Dana Roberts. She lives at 994 E. Main, right."

Surprised, Claire said, "Yes, yes it is. How'd you know?"

Marco grinned. "She's my neighbor. I think she'll be fine but we'll get her loaded into the ambulance and get her to the hospital to be sure."

"No."

Claire and Marco looked at Dana, who winced when she shook her head, but said again, "No. No hospital. I want to go home."

"You really should get checked out, Ms. Roberts," Marco said. "At least—"

"No," Dana said again. "No hospital. Help me up."

Marco helped her to her feet and guided her over to the back of the ambulance.

"She's going to be a little confused and sore for a couple of days," Marco told Claire as he checked Dana's pupils, "so I would keep an eye on her for the next forty-eight hours. If I get a chance, I may stop by myself to check on her."

Claire nodded. "Are you attached to anyone?" she asked. When Marco grinned again, she added, "Straightforward is best."

"Not attached," Marco said.

"Good, I'll take that under advisement," Claire answered, and took Dana home.

For the next two hours while Dana rested, Claire looked Marco up online, happy with what she read about him. Awards. Certificates. Recognition from the Mayor.

"I'm getting the two of you together," she said with a look toward Dana's room. "You never told me how hot this guy was, girlfriend." She shut the laptop with a snap as Dana came out of her room.

"What the hell did I trip over? I feel like I was hit with a brick."

"Girl, you tripped over a cord in the street and did a major nosedive, but that's okay. A handsome prince rescued you!"

"There are no princes. There are only toads," Dana replied, rubbing her head.

"Well be that as it may, you were rescued by that handsome prince who lives next door."

"Marco Sandoval?"

"Yeah, honey, that man's got it going on. Girl, you need to get with that. If you can't find Mr. Right, then how about Mr. Right Now?"

"Well, Mr. Right Now has never even said hello so you can just forget it."

Claire gave Dana a hug and a kiss. "Take it easy for the rest of the day. I'll finish setting up the booth for the Fest. Go rest." She pushed Dana gently toward the couch and let herself out.

Dana closed her eyes and was just falling asleep again when someone knocked. Groaning, she sat up and walked carefully to the door.

"Hi, I hope you don't mind," Marco Sandoval said when she opened it, "but I thought I had better come and check on you. You took a pretty good fall and have a couple of nasty bruises."

"It's not necessary for you to come check on me. I've been taking care of myself for quite some time."

"I'm sure you have, but this is what I do for living, and I would feel better if I checked for myself."

Realizing he wasn't going to leave until she let him see she was all right, Dana let him in and returned to the couch. Marco stood in front of her, his fingers gentle on her head.

"Ouch!" she yelped when he hit a tender spot.

"Sorry. I didn't mean to hurt you."

Dana smiled at him. "You didn't hurt me. The street did."

"You may want to go to the doctor and have that looked at."

"I'll be fine, Mr. Sandoval. Thank you for your concern."

"Just remember, if you need anything, I'm right next door."

"Yes, I know, and I'll keep that in mind." She walked him back to the door and then spent her night in a restless sleep.

Bright and early the next morning, Dana was up and ready to go, her headache almost gone.

"Not bad for a paralegal," Dana said as she walked up to the booth she and Claire were running for Fall Fest. "Looks like you've got it under control. What's left to do?"

"Just the banner." Claire unrolled the six-foot-long banner advertising Peek and Woods Law Firm in large brown letters against a cream-colored background. Dana clipped the banner to the front of the booth and stood back to admire it.

"Not bad for support staff," Claire said, and Dana laughed as their first customer came by to get all the free give away.

"So how's that neighbor of yours?" Claire asked when they had a minute again.

"Which neighbor are you referring to?"

"Why, no one other than that hunk, Mr. Sandoval."

"He's just fine. He stopped by to check on me last night, but I shooed him away," Dana replied.

"Dumb ass. You had a hot, hunky guy within two feet of you and you let him go?"

"Claire, there's no way that man, as fine as he is, is interested in me."

Claire just shook her head. "I think you're wrong. You have a lot to offer. You're bright, funny, very curvy, and extremely confident. Any man would be proud to be with you, near you or next to you."

"I'm glad you think so, but Marco Sandoval isn't interested in me."

A crowd began to form and they both got busy greeting and talking to people, handing out freebies and general information about the law firm. At about two o'clock, Dana was refilling some goodie-bags when she heard a familiar voice.

"Ms. Roberts, it's a pleasure to see you. How are you feeling?"

Dana turned, a half-full bag in her hand. Marco stood next to the booth, wearing a pair of dark-wash jeans and a white polo shirt that accentuated his muscular brown arms. Black sunglasses framed his face and held back his neck-length wavy dark hair.

"I'm doing well," Dana said. "A little sore, but I'll be fine." A small black dog with a long, fuzzy tail hopped around near Marco's feet. Bright black eyes promised mischief, and the patch of white near one of them made the dog's face irresistible. "What have you got there, Mr. Sandoval?"

"Please, call me Marco. This is my buddy Jingles." Marco reached down and scooped up the dog. "He's by my side most of the time when I'm not working."

Dana reached out and petted Jingles, who licked her hand with his quick pink tongue. "So this is the little critter who keeps digging up my flowers."

"Have you seen him doing it?"

"Just his tail." Dana laughed.

"You have time for an ice cream cone?" asked Marco.

"Oh, thank you, but I couldn't leave Claire here alone," Dana said, but Claire almost pushed her out of the booth. Giving her friend an evil look, Dana reluctantly went with Marco.

The streets were crowded with people, the greenbelt already patchworked with picnic blankets. Jingles tugged on the leash, his nose into every stray piece of trash or food he could find. After buying the ice cream cone, Dana and Marco found an empty bench. Jingles plopped down onto the sidewalk.

"So what do you do at the law firm?" Marco asked.

Dana shrugged. "Nothing spectacular. Answer phones, run errands. File stuff at the courthouse. Typing, scheduling, that sort of thing."

"All the things that would stop the office cold if you weren't there." Marco smiled.

"I guess that's right. Never thought about it that way before."

Marco's cell rang and he excused himself to answer it. Dana watched as he leaned against the wall of the hardware store, liking the easy way he moved. Finishing his conversation, he returned.

"I hate to cut this short because I'm having such a good time, but I'm needed at the station. I'm sure I'll see you in the hood."

"I'm sure you will." With a small wave, Dana returned to the booth, where Claire pounced on her the minute she got close.

"So, are you guys going to hook up or what?

"Girl, you know it was not about that. It was neighbors being neighborly."

Claire replied, "Well, we gonna have to fix that."

"Ri-i-i-ght," Dana said. A few more people crowded around their display, and from then until the evening, Dana and Claire kept busy.

"So who's the guy?" Dana nodded toward the nice-looking man in black-rimmed glasses who'd been hanging around all afternoon.

Claire whispered, "He's a new associate at one of the other firms. He asked if I wanted to go eat."

"You said yes, of course."

"Girl, are you seeing him? 'Course I said yes."

"This was fun," Dana remarked as they began to clean up their booth.

"Yeah, I got a date, and you got to converse with your extremely hot neighbor. I call that a win-win situation."

*****

Monday brought an invitation to a coworker's birthday party at one of the brand-new bars downtown on Court Avenue.

"So what do you think?" Claire asked when she called Dana. "Should we go? I know you and Melissa have this hate-hate thing going on."

"I'm surprised she even gave me an invitation. She probably expects me not to go, so I'm going just to spite her," Dana said.

Claire laughed. "It's a date."

Arriving home after work, Dana was surprised to see the package she ordered the week before sitting in her front yard with the packing slip chewed off. On Tuesday, she found her morning newspaper shredded on her front porch. The next morning, she went to get the paper and stepped right into a wet little present left for her just outside the door.

"Okay, that does it!" Hopping on one foot to get her shoe off without touching the bottom, Dana stalked down her front steps and across the lawn to Marco's house. She beat her fist a couple times against his door.

"Hey Dana, how are you?"

"Well, Mr. Marco, you and I have a little problem."

"What's going on?"

Dana shook her smelly shoe at him. "Your mutt shredded my paper and left a deposit on my porch."

"Well, Ms. Dana, I'm sorry about that but you still don't know it was Jingles."

"I have a pretty damn good idea." Dana pointed to the tiny, still wet paw prints leading from her porch steps to Marco's door.

Marco shook his head and grinned. "I'll try to keep Mr. Jingles under control."

"Hmm." Dana's eyes narrowed at his grin. Turning, she walked back to her house with as much dignity as she could find while wearing one shoe.

*****

Claire and Dana staked their claim to a good table at Toxic on Saturday night. Just about the whole office, along with their dates, had shown up for Melissa's party.

"So where's your date, Dana? I heard you have quite a cutie living next door to you."

Dana looked at the girl who'd come up behind her.

"Happy birthday, Melissa," she said quietly. "If you're referring to Marco, I didn't ask him to come. I'm sure he's busy working."

Melissa's look was almost a sneer. "You know, if you would just do a little work on yourself … but you'll never be able to reach my standards, so why try, right?"

"C'mon, Claire, let's get something to drink." Dana turned her back on Melissa, and she and Claire sipped rum punch while watching people dance.

"Hold this while I go dance with tall, dark and good-looking," Claire said, handing Dana her punch glass. Dana finished her punch and set both cups on a tray.

"Aww, poor Dana. Nobody want to dance with you?"

Melissa's nasty comment and mocking laughter followed Dana as she turned away again. At least three more times that evening, Melissa caught her unaware, each time taking a shot at her and eroding her confidence another notch.

By wandering around the club and never staying in one spot for very long, Dana finally managed to stay out of Melissa's way until almost midnight. She had just pushed the restroom door open when Melissa's voice reached her from inside.

"Did you see that ugly thing Dana was wearing?"

There was murmuring from the knot of friends who surrounded Melissa where they stood in front of the mirrors.

"Like the hired help trying to dress up," Melissa continued, and someone giggled. "She'll never amount to anything."

Dana backed off from the door, letting it close without a sound. She walked away blindly, her face burning and her stomach in knots. She had no intention of going to the bar, but when she found herself there, she slid onto a tall barstool.

"Vodka shooters," she told the bartender. "I don't care what kind. Just keep them coming."

*****

"Where are you?" Claire listened to Dana's phone ring and ring with no answer. She'd been looking for Dana for the last half hour.

"Yeah, she was here," the barkeeper said after Claire described Dana to him, "drinking Kamikazes. I'm pretty sure she's feeling no pain." He laughed.

"Idiot," Claire murmured, trying to think what to do. The firehouse! "Please be there. Please be there," she prayed as she waited for the dispatcher to find Marco. And then he was on the line.

"Claire, how can I help you?"

"Dana and I were at a party at Toxic. She was upset and left. Bartender said she had quite a few Kamikazes. She never could hold her liquor. I can't find her anywhere."

"I'm just getting off of work. I'll drive the loop and see if I can find her. Do you have any idea where she could be?"

"No, but she can't be too far. She's in high heels."

Marco barely heard Claire's 'thank you' before he was in his car and headed into downtown. He finally spotted Dana in the sculpture garden. Marco pulled over and got out of his car. Dana, one shoe off and the other in her hand, was sitting on a bench facing the street, waving at the cars and busses as they passed. Her hair had fallen from half of the clips holding it up, and her dress was hiked up to the top of her thighs.

"Slow down and come over here," Dana yelled at one of the bus drivers. "I wanna ride!"

"Dana, how 'bout I give you a ride?

"Well hey, if it isn't my extremely hot neighbor. Hiya neighbor! I'm just getting ready to ride the bus. Wanna to go with me?" Dana rose from the bench and took a step forward. The heel of her shoe stayed where it was, sunk deep into the grass, and she fell into Marco's arms.

"Why don't you let me take you home?" Marco said as he set her gently on the bench again.

"Nope, I'm going to stay here and run free like the wildebeest!" She took off her remaining shoe, throwing it on the ground. Barefoot, she ran through the garden. Marco kept one eye on her as he dialed Claire's number.

"I found her," he said when Claire answered. "We're in the sculpture park."

"Thank goodness. She okay?"

"Yeah, a little inebriated is all."

"Well, she was drinking rum punch before the Kamikazes."

Marco rolled his eyes. "That's not good."

Dana stumbled across the grass and rocks, yelling at the passing cars, her words slurred. "Why don't nobody want me?"

"I'd better get her home," Marco said.

In a couple of herding movements, he managed to get Dana near enough to his truck to get her onto the front seat. She curled up against the door, her head on the window glass. And then she began to cry.

"Dana, what's wrong?" Marco asked.

Her answer was a quiet snore

Marco pulled in front of his house and managed to get Dana inside and up to his bed. He pulled the covers over her and sat down in the chair across the room. Jingles jumped into his lap and curled up.

*****

Marco awoke the next morning as Dana stirred.

"Morning sleeping beauty," he said as he walked over and sat on the side of his bed.

"Oh God, my head," said Dana as she hid her face in the pillow.

"Tell you what. How about I go make you a hangover stopper and you can come sit at the kitchen table and drink it."

"If it'll make the pounding stop …"

"That it will. Just lay there for a few minutes and I'll be right back to help you to the kitchen."

Moment later Marco returned. Helping Dana from the bed, he guided her to the kitchen table and pushed her gently into a chair.

"Here, drink this," he said as he pushed a glass of green liquid toward her.

Dana began to cry. Marco sat down close to her and took her hand.

"What wrong sweetheart?" he asked.

"My head hurts and all night last night I had to hear my fake-ass coworker tell everybody at her birthday party all the reasons why no one is ever going to want to be with me," Dana said as her crying grew louder.

Marco reached out one strong hand and gently wiped the tears from Dana's face. "You know that is not true. There isn't a person in this whole wide world who would not want to be with you. She's just jealous."

"Then why am I still alone?" Dana wailed. "I am large and curvy and alone."

Marco took Dana into his arms and planted a gentle kiss on her forehead.

"You're a very desirable woman, Dana. Don't let anybody tell you any different. Now, drink this and let's get you home so you can go back to bed and sleep for a bit."

*****

Embarrassed over her inebriated confession to Marco, Dana spent the next two days avoiding him, going so far as to walk two blocks the other direction to keep from running into him. Her success irritated her.

"Hmph. Guess he wasn't all that worried about me after all," she muttered when he didn't come over to check on her. Deciding a little barbecue would get her mind off Marco, she fired up some chicken and steak on her grill. Twenty minutes later, she piled the meat onto a platter and set it on the small table beside her deck chair.

Returning to the kitchen, she grabbed her drink, picked up a couple napkins, steak sauce, and the knife and fork she'd also forgotten. She walked back out on the deck, where Jingles was gnawing on the last piece of chicken.

"You are soooo dead!" Dana said under her breath. Red-faced, she scooped Jingles up, marched across the lawn to Marco's house and pounded on the front door with her fist.

"Marco, your damn dog ate my dinner!"

She held Jingles, his face coated with sauce, up in the air. Marco covered his mouth, but Dana could see the smile. After a second, he burst out laughing.

"It's not funny," Dana said. She shoved Jingles at him and stormed back to her house, Marco's laughter following her. A few minutes later, her phone rang.

"Dana," Marco said, "would you like to come to dinner? It's the least I can do since my dog ate yours."

"You laughed at me."

"No, not at you. At Jingles…he had that sauce all over and…"

Dana started to smile. The dog had looked ridiculous.

"Please, Dana? Say yes."

Her voice softened. "Yes."

*****

The lights were low, the table set and candles burning. Mood music played in the background as Marco pulled out Dana's chair, put her napkin in her lap, and poured a glass of wine. Dana hardly noticed what she ate as they talked and laughed through dinner. Afterward, they sat on the floor, close but not touching, and Marco poured her another glass of wine. When he pulled her close, Dana felt like she was dreaming.

"We're going to play a game. It's called Marco Polo. I'm going to touch you, like this," and Marco ran a finger down her nose, "and if you like what I'm doing, you'll say Polo. Do we understand the rules of the game?"

"Yes," Dana said breathlessly.

Marco began as he gave her a gentle kiss on the lips.

"Polo," she said when he pulled away.

Slowly, Marco kissed his way down her neck.

Her blood heated in the places his lips touched. Her breath caught and her voice was barely audible, as she said, "Polo."

He unbuttoned her shirt, his fingers dragging lightly over each button, exposing an inch of skin at a time. When he finished, he slid his hands under the fabric, their slight roughness against her skin giving her the chills.

"Polo," Dana moaned, and then his hands were everywhere and hers explored his body the way she had wanted and needed to for longer than she could admit.

Dana couldn't talk at all anymore except to say 'Polo' to each new sensation that Marco's lips, hands and body made her feel.

"Do you want me to stop?"

"No! Please don't stop. I've dreamed about this for years."

"You are truly the most beautiful woman I have ever seen," Marco whispered in her ear. "I love your curves and every time I see you, it just makes me want you more."

Arching her back as the two of them became one, Dana rode the wave of pleasure.

Marco groaned deep in his throat. Taking Dana in his arms, he kissed her cheek and stroked her skin.

"This is not a one-time thing for me, Dana. You've been on my mind constantly. I want to be with you all the time."

With a sigh, Dana nodded against his chest.

*****

"Hey girl," Claire said when she caught up with Dana at work. "What's going on? Haven't seen you in the last couple days."

"I have something to tell you." Claire giggled.

"Oh, please tell me, girl. I'm in the mood for a good story."

"Well, I told you a couple of weeks ago I had dinner with Marco, but what I didn't tell you was not only did I have dinner, but I had dessert! "

"Are you saying what I think you're saying?"

Dana just smiled.

"I want details," Claire ordered, "and don't leave anything out."

"A real lady never tells, but we've been together every day and night since then."

The two women slapped palms and laughed, each going to her own desk. Melissa circled Dana's desk like she had something to say.

"Is there something you need?" Dana asked.

"I see your good-looking neighbor has been picking you up almost every day from work or dropping you off in the morning."

"What about it?"

Melissa gave Dana a nasty grin. "Well, inquiring minds want to know - do you really think he's something you're going to be able to keep?"

Dana stood up straight and tall and looked Melissa dead in the eye. "You have just poked the sleeping bear!"

Heads peeked over the cubicle walls and doors opened as people heard the commotion.

"What makes you think you're better than me?" Dana spit out. "What makes you think you deserve love more than me? If you spent as much time worrying about your own business and staying out of mine and everybody else's, the whole world would be better off." Dana's voice rose and her cheeks flushed, but for once she wasn't backing down. "So I'm telling you from this point on, stop fronting, because I'm tired of hearing it. This is the last earful I'm going to take from you. Go find someone else to pick on and berate, because it's not going to be me!"

Dana's watching coworkers began to clap and cheer. Over the sound of their voices, she continued, her voice firm, "Now I'm going to go deliver these papers and do my work like you should be doing, instead of rifling through everybody's desks hunting for information to use against people."

Melissa, her face red and tears welling up, stormed off. Dana calmly collected the documents she had to file at the courthouse and went outside.

Yes! I did it! Stood up to that cow and told her off. Feels pretty damn good.

The street was clear, the construction noise deafening as Dana started out from between two parked cars. A noise loud enough to shake the ground made Dana look up at the skywalk above her before her world went black.

*****

Unsure how long she'd been unconscious and wondering how she ended up flat on her back, Dana tried to get up and screamed at the searing pain. Dust and the smell of gasoline filled the air, making it hard for her to breathe. She lay there for a minute, trying to remember where she was.

"Can anyone hear me?" she called, her voice weak.

"Yes, yes, I hear you. My wife and I…we're stuck in a car, but help is on the way," a man's voice replied. "Are you hurt?"

"I - I don't know. I can't move."

The debris shifted, its weight scrunching into metal.

"Oh, my God!" A woman's voice this time. "Joe! Joe!" and then a shriek as the debris settled further.

Dana lost consciousness.

*****

"Hello? Hello!! Can you hear me?"

The voice woke Dana. Where was she? Why was…and then she remembered.

"Here. I'm here," Dana called, her voice barely reaching the rock above her head. She began to shake, goosebumps rising along her free arm. Something dripped onto her shoulder, stinging. She could hardly breathe for the fumes. Gasoline.

"Help." But her voice wasn't even a whisper. Pain crept up her body, the only thing she could feel from her chest down. The sounds of screeching metal and voices faded in and out as she struggled to stay alert and failed. Darkness crowded her mind, and she welcomed it.

*****

Bits of concrete dropped onto Dana's face, rousing her again. She choked on the dust and the gasoline fumes. Her shoulder burned with each drop that spilled onto it. Her hair became wet in the eternity she spent just trying to catch a breath. Tears pooled, overflowed. Mingled with the gas dripping onto her skin. Then light flooded down to her from an opening in the mess above her and Nick Thompson, the freckle-faced kid who'd tormented her all through grade school, peered at her.

"Oh my God! Dana is that you? Can you hear me? How bad are you hurt? Dana!"

"N-n-nick," Dana responded through chattering teeth. "C-c-cold. Sh-sh-shaking. Can't f-f-feel my body anymore."

"I'm going back up to get some more help, but we'll get you out of there."

"Don't go," she said, but the words never left her lips.

*****

Nick climbed out of the hole, his face grim. "It's the Captain's girl."

"How bad?" someone asked, and Nick shrugged.

"Don't know. Get the Cap on the radio."

"What's going on over there, Thompson?" came Marco's voice a few seconds later.

"Cap, I hate to tell you this, but Dana is one of the victims."

The radio went silent for a moment.

"She's alive. Looks like she was between two cars when the skywalk fell. That's what saved her. But, she's still caught in the debris. We got to dig her out."

"I'm on my way."

In less than five minutes, Marco strode into view, his face grey with concrete dust and exhaustion.

"Cap, she's buried completely, only her head and one arm sticking out."

Marco climbed down through the hole the crew had already made in the wreckage, his movements causing a small landslide of concrete bits and dust. Dana coughed feebly as the debris fell in her face.

"Dana," Marco said softly when he reached her. He was able to drop down next to her, but it was so tight, he could barely move. His eyes went over her rapidly, noticing a large gash on her head, a piece of glass sticking out of it. Blood streamed down her face, and the smell of gasoline was strong.

Dana opened her eyes for a second and then closed them again. Licking her dust-coated lips, she rasped out, "Hell of a way…to start our weekend."

"If you'd stop getting yourself into such trouble…" Marco's voice nearly broke. "This is a little more serious than running barefoot through the sculpture garden though."

"I always…" Her head slumped to one side.

"Dana." Marco called to her, his tone urgent. "Dana!"

"…liked pickles."

"Stay with me, baby. Just stay with me. Talk to me. Tell me what hurts."

"Cold. Cannot feel…my…anything. My leg… I think it's broken."

Shit.

"Nick, I need BP gear and a collar. Now!"

Within seconds, the crew lowered a small basket. Marco folded himself into a yoga position to get close enough to Dana to take her blood pressure, which was dangerously low.

"Sweetie, I'm need to put a cervical collar on you so we can get you out of here."

"Mmm-mmm," Dana murmured.

Trying not to move Dana's neck, Marco managed to get the collar on her. His hand came away wet and smelling of gasoline.

"Burns," Dana said.

"What burns?"

"Shoulder. Burns."

"We'll make it stop." Yelling to the men topside, he said, "I need an oxygen feed. Collar's in place. She's got a large glass shard lodged in her head. Get me a couple Kling rolls and a package of four-bys. No room for a kit down here. BP is low. Possible internal bleeding. She's in shock. How much longer till the debris is cleared?"

Nick yelled back. "One of the gas tanks ruptured. If we're not careful, the whole thing could blow."

"Yeah, I know. The shit's dripping on her."

"Crane's almost in place," Nick told him, lowering the needed supplies.

Dana was out again. Marco tugged on the oxygen line for more slack. Careful not to touch the glass, he slid the mask over her mouth and nose.

"Dana. Wake up sweetheart. You can't sleep now. Come on, Dana. Wake up."

"Just need…little n-n-nap."

"Can't let you do that, baby. You may have a concussion. You need to stay awake." While he talked, Marco bandaged her as best he could, listening with half an ear to the sounds of the crew above him working to get the lift lines in place.

"I'm tired. Head h-h-urts really bad." The oxygen seemed to be helping, putting a little more spirit into Dana as it eased her breathing. "Give me…one…good reason why I shouldn't take a nap."

Marco kept his hands moving while he answered, packing the four by four gauze squares around the glass and wrapping it all with Kling. "Because I love you with all my heart and all my soul and if you stay awake, when you get out of here you are going to marry me and Jingles."

Dana opened one eye to peer at him. "The fumes are rotting your brain." She closed her eye. "You can't be serious."

"But I am serious," Marco said, and put the last bit of wrap around her head.

"Ready up here, Cap." Nick's voice squawked through the talkie. "I'm sending the harness and board down. Let me know when you're in position."

"Roger," Marco said. He grabbed the equipment as it slid toward him, catching it before it hit Dana. He brushed a finger down her cheek.

"You with me, baby?"

"Mm-hmm."

"I'm going to get you out of here now but you're gonna have to be strong because it's going to hurt like hell."

He wormed his way around to crouch by her head, then squatting until his butt was almost on the ground, he inched the short board beneath her shoulders and back as far as he could and buckled her onto it. He slid his legs through the harness and stretched them out on either side of Dana. Using the board as a lever, he eased her into a sitting position. Dana groaned.

I hope to God I'm not cutting your spinal cord.

But there was no other way to get her out. The board was small enough to fit between them, but uncomfortable once he'd secured the harness around them both.

"Okay, Nick," he said into the talkie.

"Marco," whispered Dana, "I have to tell you something Marco, just in case I don't get out of here. I love you, too."

"I know, sweetheart. Hang on tight. I will be right here with you, and I'm not letting you go."

With a jerk and the sound of a thousand boulders crashing, the crane lifted the debris. Marco yanked Dana against him and backward. Her shriek pierced through the sounds of the moving wreckage, cutting off abruptly when she blacked out.

*****

"Who is responsible for Dana Roberts?" The doctor was young and looked as weary as Marco felt.

"That would be me. Captain Sandoval." Marco stood and clasped the doctor's hand. Claire stood next to Marco, her hands wrapped around his bicep. He could feel her fingers shaking.

"She was lucky, but she still has some major injuries. We got the glass out intact. She may have problems with headaches in the future." The doctor rubbed his hand over his face and head and around to massage the back of his neck.

"Can we see her?" Claire asked choking back her tears.

"Well, we put her into a drug-induced sleep so she'll be out for awhile but you can see her for a few minutes. We repaired her left leg and the right wrist. She had some internal bleeding. We got that stopped. She'll be here for a week or two and then we'll see what happens after that. She may need some homecare. Probably rehab. She should be back from Recovery any minute and somebody will come get you once she's back in her room."

*****

Marco and Claire took turns sitting with Dana. Marco had almost dozed off when Dana began to wake.

"Baby, I am right here with you," he said, taking her hand in his. "Dana…"

She looked at him blankly for a few seconds and then groaned when she tried to move.

"What happened? I hurt so bad."

"One of the cranes hit the side of the skywalk and brought it down. You were walking underneath when it happened."

"How long have I been out?"

"A couple days. Doc had you sedated to let your body rest."

For the next few weeks, Dana slept in between sessions with a sadistic physical therapy coach. Marco and Claire were there every day, and once she was finally released, several of her coworkers showed up to wish her a happy trip home.

"We found the perfect nurse for you," Claire said, and the other women nodded, broad smiles on their faces.

"Yeah, a reliable and caring nurse. We think you'll be very happy." Her coworkers began to giggle as they left and shut the door behind them.

Claire grinned at Dana. "I have to go back to work. Will you be okay for an hour? Your home care nurse will be here then. Just promise to behave yourself."

"With a broken leg, a broken wrist and a hole in my head, what do you think I'm going to do?"

"Just don't try to get up by yourself."

Dana eyed the walker at the side of her bed with distaste. "Don't worry, I won't."

She hadn't meant to fall asleep, but a gentle hand touching her face woke her up.

"Marco, what are you doing here?"

"I'm your home care nurse for the next three weeks." Marco grinned down at her.

"You can't do that!"

"Oh but I can and I will. You don't think I'm going to let anyone else take care of you?"

As promised, Marco took care of Dana and her every need, helping her up, making her meals, changing the bed linens and keeping her amused and occupied. Lying on the sofa at the picture window one evening just before Christmas, Dana watched the snow fall while a decorated Christmas tree sparkled in one corner of the room. The large dinner Marco had served made her doze off and on. When she awoke again, Jingles stood next to her, a card attached to the big red bow around his neck.

"What have you got there, buddy?" Dana removed the card and bow and Jingles shook himself all over, making her laugh. She opened the card.

"Merry Christmas. Turn around."

Marco stood there, dressed in red jeans, a pair of black suspenders, a Santa hat and nothing else. He was holding a small red box topped with a gold bow.

"Dana, you are the love of my life, and the only thing I think about day and night."

Bending to one knee, he opened the box and held it out toward her. Dana glanced down at the most beautiful engagement ring she'd ever seen.

"Would you do me the honor of being my wife and my love forever?"

Hobbling to her feet, Dana cried out, "Yes! Yes!"

Marco stood just in time to catch her in his arms. "Merry Christmas, my love," he said as his lips claimed hers.